THREE SCHEMES
AND A SCANDAL

Also by Maya Rodale

THREE SCHEMES
AND A SCANDAL

A Novella

MAYA RODALE

AVON IMPULSE
An Imprint of HarperCollinsPublishers

Excerpt from *A Groom of One's Own* copyright © 2010 by Maya Rodale.

Excerpt from *A Tale of Two Lovers* copyright © 2011 by Maya Rodale.

Excerpt from *The Tattooed Duke* copyright © 2012 by Maya Rodale.

Excerpt from *Seducing Mr. Knightly* copyright © 2012 by Maya Rodale.

Excerpt from *The Forbidden Lady* copyright © 2002, 2012 by Kerrelyn Sparks.

Excerpt from *Turn to Darkness* copyright © 2012 by Tina Wainscott.

EPub Edition OCTOBER 2012 ISBN: 9780062230799

Print Edition ISBN: 9780062230805

10 9 8 7 6

For Tony Coney and Penny Bunny

Part One

HASTINGS'S FOLLY

London, 1825

Prelude to a Scheme . . .

Lady Charlotte had promised: No More Schemes. Under pain of banishment to the country for the remainder of the season, as per the instructions of her beloved brother, the Duke of Hamilton and Brandon, Charlotte had solemnly vowed not to undertake any matchmaking, tempt fate, alter one's destiny or in any way meddle with the course of the universe.

Her pet fox, Penelope, would enjoy the banishment. While Charlotte found trouble wherever she went, she did so prefer London trouble. What twenty-year-old debutante would not?

In spite of Charlotte's best intentions, her last attempt to *encourage* true love (not *force*, as Brandon had said in his long, devastating lecture) had resulted in kidnapping, arson and thousands of pounds of damage to London's docks. Charlotte had not foreseen such unintended consequences. But really, who would?

She had even made a note for next time (Note to one-self: Be wary of explosions and other people's nefarious intentions). But there was to be no next time. She had promised.

Except . . .

There was the matter of Miss Lucy Fletcher. Particularly, Miss Fletcher's marital prospects, which may have been dim and which ~~were absolutely~~ may have been Charlotte's fault.

She never should have encouraged Lucy to purchase that horrid bonnet which the milliner had named *Swan Lake* because of the soft array of white plumage, shimmering blue satin ribbon and mock swan head, which curved around and arched above the brim of the bonnet. Two shiny black buttons for eyes. An orange silk beak. It was startlingly re-alistic.

Charlotte never should have suggested it would be *just the thing* to wear with Lucy's traditional white gown for the king's Swan Day celebration in Hyde Park.

It was fortunate that Charlotte had brought her parasol to beat back the swarm of angry birds that had developed an unfortunate fascination with Lucy. Charlotte risked her liberty in defense of her friend. (Killing a swan was punishable by imprisonment and death!) The so-called gentlemen about that day—the despicable Lord Dudley and his loathsome friends—laughed until they were red in the face. The other women shrieked, their cries nearly indistinguishable from the swans.

The cartoons in the newspapers were ~~hysterical~~ horrible.

Ever since, suitors were not exactly lining up to court the girl infamously known as Lucy Feathers and Swan Lucy.

Not that anyone would blame her for it, but it was Charlotte's fault for lying and telling Lucy the atrocious swan bonnet was rather fetching. Her heart impelled her to make amends.

It wouldn't do to have a perfectly lovely girl become a shriveled spinster because the bland encouragement of her friend led her into the fashion disaster of 1825.

Besides, Charlotte had the perfect remedy for Lucy's marital predicament. A scheme. And a man.

Lord Hastings's Garden Party to Commemorate His New Folly

James Beauchamp really wanted to be elsewhere. Perhaps back on the continent, from where he had returned after an extended tour (five years instead of the typical one). Perhaps back in bed with Lola, as he'd been this morning, last night and yesterday afternoon. Perhaps out at his modest country estate, enjoying the rush of a fox hunt, the thrill of galloping his stallion across the fields or simply a long stroll without the stuffiness of his jacket and cravat.

Instead he was stuck at this loathsome garden party to celebrate a *folly*. Not only would he have to give a speech later, at exactly four o'clock, about the significance of the useless structure his father had designed, but he was stuck socializing as The Dutiful Son while Gideon, The Favored Son, was securing world peace at the European courts.

James maintained a conversation with Lady Something Or Other, who was past her prime yet did not behave as such. She was throwing herself at him, as women were wont to do.

"Mr. Beauchamp, James. You don't mind if I call you James, do you?" She purred this at him, slinking one finger along the arm of his jacket. He resisted a shudder.

"Your scar, James, is just so . . . dashing," she cooed. The damned scar . . . the women loved it so he really couldn't complain. But they would not think it so dashing if they knew the true source of that fine slash that graced his left cheek.

"Tell me, James, how did you suffer such an injury?"

James pushed his fingers through his hair and adopted a grave expression.

"A broken shard of glass wielded by a madman who had escaped from Bedlam. I was defending a blind, eight-year-old girl from his murderous clutches," James said. It was a lie. The stories were always outrageous falsehoods. The truth could not be spoken aloud.

Lady Whatever sighed and clasped her bosom. He could have her, if he wanted.

Across the ballroom, James set his sights on Lady Charlotte Brandon. He hadn't seen her in an age. He discovered now that she had become beautiful. Dark hair, alabaster skin, a wicked smile on her red lips. He wondered if she was still the same troublesome, maddening minx.

He did not intend to find out.

The Terrace

As always, Charlotte enlisted the assistance of her dearest friend, Miss Harriet Dawkins. The two young ladies—one tall and dark haired, the other short and freckled—linked arms and strolled across Lord Hastings's terrace en route to the lemonade table. Presently guests were milling about, enjoying refreshments and gossip.

Charlotte overheard Lord and Lady Capulet avidly recounting the dramatic construction and redecoration of their new library. Lady Layton flirted shamelessly with Lord Beaverbrook while her husband stood nearby, admiring a topiary.

Swan Lucy stood with her mother, talking to other matrons and their wallflower daughters. Soon, Swan Lucy would be married to the dashing James Beauchamp and she'd have Charlotte to thank for it. One day, years later, they would name their firstborn daughter Charlotte in gratitude to the enterprising young miss who brought them together.

But first, the scheme . . .

"Is everything ready, Harriet?" Charlotte asked in a hushed, conspiratorial whisper. Then she smiled a smile that suggested she was nothing but an innocent young lady happily attending a garden party.

"I have the key in my reticule. But please, remind me how this is supposed to work?" Harriet asked in a nervous voice. If Charlotte possessed nerves of steel, Harriet's were constructed of delicate gossamer strung from a violet on a dewy morning.

Charlotte did not reply. They had reached the refreshments table, which was crowded with guests who might overhear and attempt to stop her Noble Efforts at True Love.

Instead, Charlotte ladled two glasses of lemonade, taking care for her new dress—a fetching cream-colored muslin with delicate lace cap sleeves, daringly cut low in the front *and* the back. The bodice was adorned with more lace, handmade by fallen women residing in a convent in Belgium.

Darling as it was, white dresses were *such* a bother. When she was married she would always wear dark colors, which were far better suited for sneaking out at midnight.

Presumably.

Having obtained their lemonades, they slipped away to a private corner of the terrace. Charlotte took a sip and explained the day's scheduled events:

"To start, a footman will approach James at three o'clock about a problem at the folly that requires his immediate attention."

"What is the problem?" Harriet asked, blinking, perplexed.

"There is no problem. Which means it will take him forever to find it, affording us more time to enact the second aspect." Charlotte smiled wickedly.

"Then what happens?"

"We casually mention to Swan Lucy that James has gone off to the folly for a private preview with a select group. And then we invite her to join us. Of course she'll say yes," Charlotte explained. "Anyone would."

"Who is the select group?" Harriet asked.

"You, me and Lucy."

"That is incredibly select," Harriet remarked. "Shouldn't we have a chaperone?"

"We'll all chaperone each other," Charlotte replied, although the whole point was to allow James and Lucy unchaperoned time together. One could not possibly fall in love with a dowager or giggling friend looking over her shoulder. "Next, once we are inside the folly, you and I shall slip off and lock them in. Then they will proceed to fall in love. Or something."

For some unusual reason the prospect of James falling in love with Lucy elicited a fleeting pang of angst. Nothing to call the doctor about, though. Charlotte ignored it. Her nerves were those of steel, coated in iron and bolstered by stone.

Charlotte spied James across the terrace. He was deep in conversation with Lady Whitmore, who was an exceedingly merry widow. Charlotte wondered if they . . .

No, no she didn't. She was going to play Cupid and fix him up with her friend who would otherwise die a spinster because of Charlotte's dreadful fashion advice. She didn't wonder anything about him and she especially did not wonder about kissing him or anything of the sort.

In 1817 she had banished him from her heart forevermore.

Presently, however, she did suffer another pang. Of longing? Of jealousy? Of a fatal heart ailment?

"How long?" Harriet asked.

"How long does it take them to fall in love?" Charlotte echoed. "Oh, I suppose a quarter of an hour should do the trick."

"No, how long do we leave them in the folly?" Harriet corrected. She clutched her reticule tightly. The key to the folly was securely tied in with a ribbon for if it were lost . . .

Charlotte would somehow procure another one. Surely the butler had a spare and would quietly relinquish it. That's what pin money was for, after all.

"Oh, well James is scheduled to speak at four o'clock. So we must unlock the door before that. Then we shall join the group at the folly, listen to the speech and all live happily ever after."

"Perhaps they shall be so grateful to us that they'll name their firstborn daughter Harriet," Harriet said.

"Perhaps," Charlotte murmured through pursed lips, as a gentle breeze stole over the garden, rustling leaves and setting bonnet ribbons aflutter.

Most young ladies spent their pin money on hats and hair ribbons; Charlotte spent hers on bribery.

At precisely three o'clock Charlotte sipped her lemonade and watched as a footman dressed in royal blue livery approached James with the unfortunate news that something at the folly needed his immediate attention.

James raked his fingers through his hair—she thought it best described as the color of wheat at sunset on a harvest day. He scowled. It did nothing to diminish his good looks. Combined with that scar, it only made him appear more brooding, more dangerous, more rakish.

She hadn't seen him in an age. Not since George Coney's funeral.

Even though the memory brought on a wave of sadness

and rage, Charlotte couldn't help smiling broadly when James set off for the folly at a brisk walk. Her heart began to pound. The plan was in effect.

Just a few minutes later, the rest of the garden party gathered round Lord Hastings as he began an ambling tour of his gardens, including vegetable gardens, a collection of flowering shrubs and a series of pea-gravel paths that meandered through groves of trees and other landscaped "moments."

Charlotte and Harriet skulked toward the back of the group, studiously avoiding relatives—such as her brother and his wife, Sophie, who were watching Charlotte a little too close for comfort ever since The Scheme That Had Gone Horribly Awry. Harriet's mother was deep in conversation with her bosom friend, Lady Newport.

A few steps ahead was Miss Swan Lucy herself. Today she was decked in a pale muslin gown and an enormous bonnet that had been decorated with what seemed to be a shrubbery. Upon closer inspection it was a variety of fresh flowers and garden clippings. Even a little bird (fake, one hoped) had been nestled into the arrangement. Two wide, fawn-colored ribbons tied the millinery event to her head.

Charlotte felt another pang and then—Lord Above—she suffered *second thoughts*. First the swan bonnet, and now this! James had once broken her heart horribly but could he really marry someone with such atrocious taste in bonnets? And if not, should the scheme progress?

"Lovely day for a garden party, is it not?" Harriet said brightly to Miss Swan Lucy.

"Oh indeed it is a lovely day," Lucy replied. "Though it would be so much better if I weren't so vexed by these bonnet strings. This taffeta ribbon is just adorable, but immensely itchy against my skin."

"What a ghastly problem. Try loosening the strings," Charlotte suggested. Her other thought she kept to herself: *Or remove the monstrous thing entirely.*

"It's a bit windy. I don't wish it to blow away," Harriet said nervously. Indeed, the wind had picked up, bending the hat brim. On such a warm summer day such as this, no one complained.

"A gentle summer breeze. The sun is glorious, though," Harriet replied.

"This breeze is threatening to send off my bonnet and I shall freckle terribly without it in this sun. Alas!" Lucy cried, her fingers tugging at her bonnet strings.

"What is wrong with freckles?" Harriet asked. The correct answer was *nothing*, since Harriet herself possessed a smattering of freckles across her nose and rosy cheeks.

"We should find you some shade," Charlotte declared. "Shouldn't we, Harriet?"

"Yes. Shade. Just the thing." Harriet was frowning, probably in vexation over the comment about freckles. Charlotte thought there were worse things, like being the featherbrain that Lucy was.

Charlotte suffered another pang. She loathed second thoughts and generally avoided them. She reminded herself that while James had once been her favorite person in England, he had since become the sort of man who brooded endlessly and flirted heartlessly.

Never mind what he had done to George Coney.

"We might steal away to the folly. James—Mr. Beauchamp,

that is—offered Harriet and me a private tour. Would you like to join us?"

"Oh!" Lucy exclaimed. And then the magnitude of the invitation seemed to register: an opportunity to be with one of London's most eligible bachelors. Also, there would be shade. She might remove her bonnet and not suffer freckles.

"I'll take that as a yes. Come along!" Charlotte led the way down a pea-gravel path that crunched under their satin slippers. The sun was shining warmly. The birds were chirping pleasantly. A strong breeze ruffled through the garden. A scheme was in the works—second thoughts be darned. The folly loomed ahead of them: a circular stone structure with pillars and trellises ready for climbing branches of wisteria. The building itself evoked an ancient Roman structure, complete with deliberate signs of "distress" such as an artfully arranged pile of stones or patches of moss nurtured among the rocks.

And then everything went wrong.

The Folly

There was nothing wrong with the damned folly. James had not believed the footman when he said so, but he had welcomed the opportunity to escape the party. He was at heart a wild man, made for roaming the countryside from atop a galloping horse, not strolling at a snail's pace through a garden clipped and manicured within an inch of its life. James preferred the raucous atmosphere of a country pub to a London party. His taste was for lusty, loving women not simpering misses. He also thought a building—or a man—ought to have a purpose.

Damned folly.

Damned Gideon, off kissing arse in foreign courts using any one of the seven languages he spoke fluently—not that he could say something interesting in any of them. His elder brother was a part of a select envoy of ambassadors to the continent, appointed directly by the king. Their father only mentioned this, oh, in every other breath.

Their father's other favorite topic was architecture; or, as James thought of it: math and rocks. Unfortunately that was not an appropriate sentiment to share in the speech honoring his father's architectural accomplishments, due to be delivered at precisely four o'clock this afternoon. Most unfortunately, that was all he had prepared.

The main use of this folly is to demonstrate how math and stones can work together to create a structure with no point whatsoever.

The speech was doomed. He had tried to prepare by studying the extensive collection of literature on follies to be found in the Hastings library. James even read a few of his father's articles in *The Exhaustive Digest of Architecture in England*. The problem was that James fell asleep every time he tried to read them. It was the dull subject matter, to be sure, the dim light in the library, the stifling air . . .

For once—just once—it would be nice to do something for which his father could be proud of him. Oh, he had his talents: taming horses, fox hunting, starting fires, winning all manner of races or feats of physical strength, bringing women to the brink of such pleasure as they had never known . . .

But these were not things for which his father would be proud of him.

No, James must deliver a thoughtful, informed, poignant speech of this damned folly at four o'clock today or consider himself disowned.

In the Garden

Charlotte had not factored in the weather. In particular, she had not considered the physics of wind, and a wide-brim, unsecured bonnet. Such were the failings of a Proper Lady's education.

A particularly robust gust launched Lucy's bonnet, cresting on the wind, right up into a tree, where it became entangled in the branches just out of reach.

"My bonnet!" Lucy shrieked.

Charlotte swore softly under her breath, as one did in such situations. It was so vexing when plans went awry. But one had to adapt. She swiftly examined the options:

~~Abandon the monstrosity.~~

Charlotte might climb the tree to rescue it. Climbing trees was all the rage these days, thanks to daring escapades of *The London Weekly*'s advice columnist, Dear Annabelle. Charlotte could do it—she had learned from James ages ago—but it was unlikely her delicate white dress would survive unscathed.

They could go fetch a gallant gentleman for assistance or . . .

"Lucy, why don't you go to the folly and see if perhaps

there is a rake we might use to retrieve the bonnet," Charlotte suggested.

She could not help but smirk at her own wit. Lucy would think the rake would refer to a garden implement, when actually Charlotte meant James. Tussled hair, deep blue eyes, rakish James.

"Ugh, I wouldn't want to go in there," Lucy said, glancing warily at the folly and then longingly at her bonnet.

"Why not?" Charlotte asked.

"It's probably dusty and dirty and full of old bones." Lucy punctuated this with a delicate shudder.

"It's a folly, not a mausoleum. Furthermore, it's new. Which is why we are here today. To celebrate a clean, new building," Charlotte said.

After standing aside and seriously considering the problem, Harriet's expression brightened. "I know!" she exclaimed.

Charlotte tilted her head, curious, and then her eyes widened with horror as Harriet's plan became apparent.

Harriet tossed her reticule—*with the key to the folly*—up at the stuck hat in an attempt to free it, however she only managed to prove Newton wrong. What went up did not necessarily come down.

Charlotte groaned, her voice trailing off as she watched Lucy Featherbrains attempt to solve the problems of a hat and a reticule stuck in a tree.

She started to hop in a delicate attempt to reach her stupid bonnet. When that was hopeless, she lifted her skirts and jumped, crouching down low before popping up high. Such efforts were to no avail.

Lucy resorted to lifting her skirts past her knees—Lord

help them all if any gentleman should happen upon them—sprinting and leaping into the air.

The bonnet was nearly within her grasp!

And then poor Lucy landed not on the soft grass but on a knobby tree root, which caused her to set down at an awkward and painful angle. And then she collapsed. On the ground.

"Oh! My ankle!"

"Oh no!" Harriet said, rushing to her side. "Here, let me help you."

"I'll go get a blasted rake," Charlotte mumbled as she stomped off to the folly. She would get James to help fetch the troublesome hat and to help carry the troublesome Lucy back to the party.

The scheme was ruined.

Toward the rear of the building was a heavy wooden door. She pushed it open and stepped inside the cool, circular room. Light and wind filtered in from open windows placed high on the walls, almost near the ceiling.

Another evil gust of wind blew the door shut. It swung easily on its new, well-oiled hinges. The lock clicked ominously.

To make matters worse, she heard the sound of an iron latch on the outer door jarred loose as it slid into its holder, probably owing to the force with which the door slammed closed.

Charlotte couldn't help but wonder if doors locked in a way other than ominously. Perhaps securely. Which meant that she was securely and ominously ensconced in the folly.

With a rake.

James leaned against the folly wall, perched on a stack of old wooden crates. His arms were folded across his broad chest. He did not smile.

"Lady Charlotte Brandon. Causing trouble once again," he remarked in the cool voice of a practiced rogue.

"Mr. James Beauchamp. Be still my beating heart," she retorted. But really, if only her heart would *slow down*. It wasn't as if she hadn't been alone with James before or even in trouble with James. Granted, they had been children at the time.

James was very much a man now. All large, muscled and overbearing. He glanced down at her as if she were still a naughty child. Nothing irked Charlotte more than being underestimated. People did so at their own peril. As James would soon discover.

And yet she stood straighter, arched her back slightly and adopted a haughty expression.

"Dare I even ask why we are locked in this folly together?" James questioned.

"You presume this was planned," she replied, tipping her chin higher.

"Are you familiar with your reputation?" he questioned and she gave him a sickly sweet smile in response.

"Oh yes: Sparkling conversationalist, pretty and exquisite manners even with the most boorish company," she replied.

James leaned forward, his blue eyes focused upon hers.

"Or: Too clever for her own good. Devious. Destructive. Dangerous." His voice positively caressed the words— *Devious. Destructive. Dangerous.* He couldn't possibly be talking about her. No, he had to be describing himself.

Also, he did not deny that she was pretty. Which mattered more than she liked. Once again, she willed her racing heart to slow to a less missish pace.

"My goodness. I cannot tell which appeals to me more," Charlotte said lightly when, in fact, her heart was pounding. "Devious? Or dangerous?"

"Trouble. Definitely trouble," James muttered.

"If you must know, I came here seeking a rake," she said haughtily. She did not want him to think she had planned this encounter. Truth be told, she hadn't planned to be alone with him. She was remembering why: James did not buy her act.

"You found one," he replied dryly. This pun had amused her before, but it irked her now. Or was it James? He, once so wild and carefree, was now some sardonic, know-it-all rake who lamentably was making her nerves tingle and pulse race.

"Miss Fletcher's bonnet is stuck in a tree," Charlotte offered as an explanation.

"Horrors," he said, with a deadpan expression.

She couldn't help it, a grin tugged at her lips. "You would think so by the way she carries on. Apparently there is no fate worse than freckles."

"We had better rescue her bonnet then," James said, standing up and towering above her. From his evergreen wool jacket to the tips of his shiny Hessians, he was every inch the gentleman. Yet his cheeks were sun-browned and his boots, upon closer inspection, were actually worn. She imagined him hiking across his land, surveying all he possessed, perhaps rescuing a damsel in distress, or helping a neighbor repair a fence.

James was no city dandy, certainly. If anyone could procure

Swan Lucy's bonnet from its captivity in the tree branches, it was he.

To hell with the bonnet. Charlotte, inexplicably, did not want to leave the folly.

If there were worse fates than being locked in a small, dim chamber with Charlotte, James could not think of them. It was generally impossible to think straight around Charlotte. She'd always been a veritable hurricane of outrageously terrible ideas. She had more courage than a girl ought to and an impish smile that made it impossible to admonish her.

He discovered today that she possessed far more dangerous, womanly charms than her smile. She was by all rights the same daring girl, but with the figure of a siren, a gleam of mischief in her pretty blue eyes, milky white skin and the delicate features of a demure English maiden that was lies, all lies.

When had this transformation occurred?

He hadn't been in London long, hadn't spent much of that time at ton parties and definitely had not associated with marriageable misses when he had. Still, James knew the rumors: Charlotte would be considered a catch—for her generous dowry and pretty looks—if only it were less work to keep up with her.

Most men did not have the fortitude for a woman like her, James included.

Especially today.

Especially when he was due to give a speech about an architectural farce before London Society and his ever-disapproving father. Just once, he had thought while shaving this morning, just once he'd like to make the old man proud.

Now he'd evermore be referred to as the son who idiotically got himself locked in a folly at an afternoon garden party.

"What time is it?" he asked.

"You're the one with the timepiece," she pointed out. He scowled. And checked.

"A quarter after three," he said. "I am due to make a speech at four o'clock."

"Ah, yes. When the entire garden party assembles before this very folly so that we might enjoy a lengthy lecture upon the features of this marvelous impenetrable fortress and the architectural design talents of Lord Hastings, all illuminated by his devoted son. I trust you have practiced."

"Perhaps it's better if I am locked in here until nightfall," James muttered.

"We will be discovered eventually," Charlotte said consolingly. But then her eyes widened in alarm and some awful truth dawned. "And then we will have to marry!"

In unison, both Charlotte and James lunged for the door, vainly grasping the brass knob and turning it every which way. They rattled the heavy door on its freshly oiled hinges, finding it expertly measured, cut and hung so that it fit snugly in the frame and would not budge.

"The footman said there was a problem with the folly. I had no idea it was the blasted lock," James muttered, rattling the knob once more.

"Well the lock certainly isn't broken. In fact, it seems to be in excellent working order. Alas."

"Thank you Charlotte, that is so helpful."

"You are so welcome, James. Fear not, I shall find a way out for us," Charlotte said.

She raised her fist high and opened her mouth wide to holler for help when James realized he had to act suddenly to stop her from making a grave mistake. With one hand he grabbed her wrist, just as she was about to pound on the door. He clamped his other hand, palm down, over her mouth before she shrieked for help, bringing the attention of God only knew who upon them.

He spun her around swiftly so her back was against the door. He held her trapped, captive, between his body and the door, with her wrist locked in his grip and pinned above her head. Her mouth pressed against his palm and the slightest *mmm* escaped her soft lips. She wriggled against his restraint, her hips writhing against him. She arched her back, jutting her breasts forward.

He forgot about the folly.

He thought only of her luscious curves and how he wanted to thoroughly explore them. Given how he held her, she had little room to protest. His arousal was now straining for more, and it occurred to James that he could tug up her skirts, part her legs slightly more and bury himself within her. He'd show her danger. Trouble.

There was no fear in Charlotte's eyes.

Damn. He would *not* find this erotic. Not here, not now, not *Charlotte*.

"Do not make a sound," he rasped, his voice betraying how hard he was and how much he wanted her.

She mewled in protest against his palm.

"We must escape and we must not draw attention to ourselves while doing so. We have about forty minutes to accomplish this. Do you understand?" James asked. She nodded solemnly.

He released her.

"Who designed this thing to lock like this?" she asked, sounding peevish.

"My father," James answered.

She glanced around the folly, taking in what little of it there was. A stone tower, devoid of anything but a pile of wooden crates. "I suppose he is also the one who placed the windows so high up. You'd think there's buried treasure in here or something," she remarked.

He caught that gleam in her eye, and he just knew that she was concocting tales of long-dead pirates burying a fortune in stolen treasure *in the middle of London*. James decided that a dose of logic was required to combat the madness in her brain.

"It's to control the temperature and air circulation. Hot air rises, and then escapes and . . ." James's voice trailed off as he realized that perhaps he had internalized more of the architectural lectures he'd read than previously realized.

"Treasure would be so much better," Charlotte said and he thought of the time when she had been absolutely convinced that an ancient Brandon family treasure had been buried underneath her mother's heirloom rose garden.

The excavation had not been successful. The punishment had been severe.

You should know better his father had lectured. *Idiot boy.* Then the belt came out.

"There's no treasure, Charlotte. None at all," James said impatiently. "Although I can think of something far better."

"Feeling the sunlight on our cheeks, and cool breeze in our hair. In other words, not being locked in here at all?"

"Exactly. Give me one of your hairpins," James said. Being Charlotte, she didn't ask *why*. She simply reached up and tugged out a pin and handed it to him, saying:

"This is my lucky lock-picking pin." She smiled. A wisp of her dark hair, now unrestrained, tumbled down, grazing her shoulder.

He forced himself to look away and set to work on the lock.

"I hope you have improved in your lock-picking skills since the summer we were spies," Charlotte said.

"Pretended," James corrected. "We were seven and ten years of age. I don't think any government recruits children to do such dirty work."

"1812 was a splendid year. We picked locks, wrote in code and skulked around Hamilton Manor," she said.

"And we were soundly punished for troubling the staff and assuming your butler, Gerard, was a spy for the French," James reminded her.

"I'm still not convinced he wasn't," she replied breezily.

"Damn it," James swore. The pin broke. She handed him another two.

He was vaguely aware of her strolling about the folly—which required a grand total of twenty paces in a circle. Her hair, dark and luscious, tumbled about her shoulders. Her hairpins were broken in the lock.

"Do you happen to carry a pistol, perchance?" Charlotte asked.

"Funny, it didn't cross my mind to bring one to an afternoon garden party," he replied.

"Pity, that. We could simply shoot the lock off," she said with a shrug.

"And cause a horrible racket that would draw the attention of two hundred guests touring the garden. They would probably not let us out until a special license and vicar were obtained and put to use."

"Perish the thought. Let me try," she said, sinking to her knees on the folly floor. She wrinkled her nose, bit her lip and furrowed her brow as she wriggled the pin this way and that until . . .

Click!

She tried the doorknob, which easily twisted. Her triumphant smile faded when it was clear the door would still not open.

"That damned latch," they both muttered in unison.

If it weren't for that damned latch they might be free. One would think his father *was* planning to stash an ancient treasure in this damned folly, given the level of security installed in a decorative garden structure.

"Do you have a knife? We could just saw through and . . ." Charlotte said, her voice faltering. The latch was iron. A knife would be useless.

"No, I don't have a knife. Or a pistol, a sword or a bow and arrow—"

Charlotte's eyes brightened considerably at the mention of her favorite weaponry. Lord, help them all.

"I haven't shot since—"

"The day you nearly shot my eye out?" he finished for her. Oh, the memories. He traced his finger along the slash of the scar that graced his left cheek.

"Since the day we dramatically reenacted William Tell," she replied smartly. "If you hadn't had an attack of nerves and moved your head, I would have gotten the apple. As it was, my arrow only just grazed your cheek."

"Leaving me horribly disfigured," he said, mainly to rile her up.

"Leaving you with a dashing scar that I know you use to impress the ladies," Charlotte corrected. "I have heard on the best authority that you received that scar from a duel over a milkmaid's virtue, during a pirate attack while crossing the Channel and during a brutal interrogation at the Bastille."

"I couldn't very well tell them I was shot by a twelve-year-old girl," James replied.

"Nor could you tell them the truth, which is that you stepped into the path of a twelve-year-old girl's arrow," she retorted. Maddeningly. "Honestly, all I can say is you're welcome."

"I beg your pardon?" His jaw might have dropped open.

"I could have told everyone the truth. But instead I allowed all those nitwit ladies to persist in believing your ridiculous version of events. As I said, you're welcome."

Charlotte was . . . Charlotte. She was devious and dangerous, maddening, exasperating. The damned thing was, she looked so pretty while she turned your world upside down. But then one had to endure punishment and lectures and go to great lengths to repair all the damage her clever ideas had wrought.

And if they did not escape this folly soon, she would be his maddening, devious and dangerous wife.

He felt exhausted merely thinking about the possibility.

James dared a glance at her and his heart stopped in his throat. Her hair was a dark tussled mess, as if a man had run his fingers through it while savagely making love to her. There were two dirty stains on her white gown at knee height, the result of her kneeling on the ground to pick the lock. Not that anyone would believe *that*. No, they would think she'd been kneeling for something else entirely.

This was bad. This was worse than bad.

"We need to get out of here," he said firmly. "Quickly, and unnoticed."

"The windows," Charlotte said resolutely. The windows were seven feet from the ground, but they were their only option.

Then, oddly, James was glad to be suffering this scheme with Charlotte. Any other girl would be having an attack of the vapors, where as she . . . Dear God, what was she undertaking now?

While James woolgathered, Charlotte began arranging the crates into a suitable tower for climbing to reach the windows. He quickly stepped in to help, lifting them high with an ease that made her think of his muscles flexing taut and strong underneath his clothes.

This inspired all sorts of ridiculous imaginings: James, working in naught but his shirtsleeves on a hot summer day, perhaps cooling off by pouring a bucket of cold water over his head, plastering his wet, transparent shirt to the hard, defined planes of muscles of his chest.

The imagination was a wicked, wanton tease. The imagination also caused her to feel lightheaded, which made her think of fainting into his arms. Dear Annabelle's latest column in *The London Weekly* had suggested the very thing as a way to attract a man's attention.

"You know, Charlotte, it's funny that you didn't ask me why I was in the folly," James remarked.

Actually, she wanted to correct him: It wasn't funny at all. Most of the ton unwittingly participated in her schemes without question. Today she had to tangle with a smart one.

"Let's say that I was rather preoccupied with getting out of here," she replied.

"Nevertheless, I can't help but wonder if this is one of your schemes," James said, glancing sideways at her.

"I wasn't planning for *us* to be stuck here," she replied and wasn't that the truth!

"Really? This is not some scheme to entrap me in a lifetime of matrimony?"

"You think highly of yourself. No, James, if you must know you broke my heart in 1817 and I haven't quite forgiven you for it."

Had she really just said that? Of course. She'd been waiting eight years to let him know of the hurt he caused her.

"What happened in 1817?" She watched as James did the math to calculate their ages, and searched the far recesses of his memory for an event of such devastating magnitude occurring when she was twelve and he fifteen. His brow furrowed. And then he remembered.

"Because I wouldn't attend a funeral for your pet rabbit?" he asked.

"Our rabbit, George Coney. It wasn't just that you wouldn't attend, but you mocked me for it. In front of everyone. And—"

"I was an idiot lad of fifteen and had schoolmates around for the holiday," James explained in one of those carefully cultivated patient voices which she used when she spoke to her toddler cousins.

"—And then," Charlotte said, her voice rising as she recollected The Horrible Thing They Did, "you and your idiot friends ate him!"

She had invited James to join her for George Coney's funeral. After all, they had discovered the injured rabbit together six years earlier. Together, they had nursed the poor thing back to health. George had been her beloved pet, and James her beloved friend and partner in crime.

But James had grown too old for her games, and he had laughed at her along with his schoolmates. But then the body of her beloved pet went missing. And then the body was discovered. Roasting. On a spit. On the front lawn of Hastings House.

"Dudley did it," James maintained. "And he is an idiot and I am no longer friends with him. I did not partake in George Coney."

"I thought I was your friend," she said softly. She had been hysterical, inconsolable. She still had not forgiven Dudley or James.

Charlotte could articulate now what she could not then. She had been devastated by the loss of her pet, which she had rescued—with James's assistance—from the garden. More so, she had been stung by the sudden loss of her best friend who suddenly, after one term at Eton, wanted nothing to do with her. She could understand the mocking and the reluctance to associate with a girl, she supposed. Worst of all, he had traded her company for a pet-eater like Dudley.

Charlotte knew now that it was a stupid thing boys and men did—deny feelings and sensitivity and resort to extraordinary lengths to prove they had hearts of stone.

She could forgive James all that, if she were a better person. Occasionally she had moments. But she could not forgive the way he never really spoke to her again after that incident. Had their years of friendship meant nothing?

"Have you been holding this grudge for eight years?"

It wasn't as if he gave her a chance to forgive him. He never asked her to turn about the room, or waltz, or offered to fetch her lemonade. All those little gestures signified nothing to anyone else but would have meant the world to her. She didn't say that, though.

"I was going to set you up with a very nice young lady," Charlotte said. "But her bonnet became entangled in tree branches."

"I have narrowly escaped matrimony to one girl, only to find myself risking it with another," James remarked.

"I don't want to be here either, James. And I certainly don't want to marry someone who mocks delicate young ladies when they are in a fragile emotional state, quite possibly eats pets and then refuses to speak to their childhood friend for eight years," she said, pausing to turn and face him. He shrugged—how infuriating! "In other words, you. I don't want to marry you," she added.

Really, though, she didn't want to entrust her heart to him again, knowing he might forsake her. Again.

"I got that," he said leveling a stare. His eyes were very

blue, and she was all in awe of his gaze as he took her in: tussled girl, dirty dress. She must have looked like a petulant child. Except there was nothing childlike about the way he looked at her, or how it made her feel.

"Well, say something," Charlotte implored after he stared at her for a long while.

Then James grinned, tugged one of her curls and said, "C'mon, Char, let's get the hell out of here. I'm going to climb up on those crates and see if I can reach the window."

Like that, the moment was over, yet a hint of their old familiarity had resurfaced.

"It would mean so much to me if your first act of freedom was to unlatch the door. I'd have the devil of a time explaining to my brother why I was locked in a folly," she said.

"I'm sure you would manage magnificently. I'm also sure he wouldn't be surprised in the slightest."

"I'm not sure if that is a compliment. Or not."

"I know you, Charlotte," murmured James. He did, like no one else. Even Harriet. She was used to being misunderstood or avoided by those scared of her reputation for wit and trouble. With those warm words, with that heated look, a little bit of her loneliness melted.

"What time is it?" she asked.

"A quarter to four!" James said. Then he swore, viciously. And she grinned, wickedly.

"Perhaps we needn't be out by four precisely. We can wait until after everyone leaves and then presumably a servant will return here for something. Thus, we shall obtain our freedom and his silence for a nominal fee. Servants are easily bribed. Don't ask how I know that."

"I am due to give a speech honoring my father and commemorating the completion of this folly. I must also do so up to the standards of the oh-so-perfect Gideon."

"Well you'd better see to climbing out that window then," Charlotte urged. If Gideon was half as insufferable as he'd been as a child . . . She supposed people like Gideon served a useful purpose in the world, such as taking on tedious tasks no one else wanted, and serving as excellent people to prank.

"See if Harriet is outside. We can call for her."

James climbed up the crates, reaching for the window and pulling his weight up enough so he could peer out.

"I don't see Harriet."

"She must have helped Lucy back to the party."

"Your plans have failed spectacularly, Charlotte," James said, adopting a tragic expression.

"Yes my plan for you to climb out the window and unlock the door is not going as planned."

"About that . . ."

"What? Why are you climbing down?" Charlotte asked, a note of panic creeping into her voice. The clock was literally ticking, time was running out and she was facing *exile!*

"Oh damn," James swore. In his haste to return to the ground, James's breeches caught on a nail jutting from a crate. The couple fell silent at the sound of ripping fabric.

Two pairs of blue eyes nervously looked down to the gentleman's lower half, which was indelicately exposed thanks to a tear along the breeches, exposing his unmentionables.

"Your jacket will cover it," Charlotte said and it was mostly the truth. The tear was positioned such that, so long as he didn't move or bend over, or if the wind didn't blow the tails of his coat, no one would notice. "Hurry."

"Also . . ." James began in a tone a voice that was a prelude to something not good.

"*Also?*" Charlotte echoed, infusing more drama than necessary into the syllables.

"I don't think I'll be able to climb out the window. Can't get high enough. But I could lift you, then you could shimmy down and go unlatch the door."

"In skirts?"

"Take them off," James said with a shrug.

Her mouth dropped open. Even she, the ever-unflappable Charlotte Brandon, was shocked by a gentleman's simple command to disrobe before him.

And then to climb out a window at a garden party.

In her underthings.

This was a bit much, even for her, which was really saying something.

"I beg your pardon!" she said, because it seemed the thing to say in such a situation. If her brother found out about this, she would be packed off to Scotland by midnight. Perhaps even Australia.

"Charlotte, we are a facing a lifetime of —"

"Holy matrimony? Wedded bliss? Eternal devotion?"

"Take your damned dress off," he growled, eyes flashing.

"Bloody hell," she swore.

"Language, young lady," he reprimanded.

"Now you develop a sense of propriety," she retorted.

"If only you would have done so an hour ago, we wouldn't be in this mess."

"Oh!" Charlotte pressed her palms against his rather hard chest and pushed him. He stumbled back a step, because he was startled and not because of the force. His hands closed around her wrists and he held her. Close. Then, he turned her around.

Suddenly, it became difficult to breathe, as she was held flush against him and aware that he was aroused by this. If the heat in her belly—and lower—was any indication, she was too.

Obviously, there was a design flaw with the air supply in the folly. James ought to mention that in his speech. His speech!

"How much time do we have?" Charlotte asked, sounding more breathless than she would have liked.

"I'm not really watching the clock right now, Charlotte," James said. His voice was strangely husky and it did things to her. Made her feel things.

And then he began to unbutton her dress. He worked quickly, and the speed, ease and determination with which he divested her of her gown were anything but seductive.

Or so she told herself.

She had felt his fingertips brush quickly and gently against her bare skin, where no man had ever touched her. She had felt the pause when he had undone all the buttons, but hadn't moved to help her out of the gown. As if he were looking, drinking her in.

Charlotte stepped out of her dress and looked for a place to hang it. She settled for the knob of the door. That cursed, locked door.

"Are you ready?" James asked her. His eyes had darkened. They focused firmly on her face. And it irritated her that a rake such as he did not openly ogle her. One lascivious stare was the least he could give her.

"Of course," she replied, as if she stripped down to her undergarments in front of gentlemen regularly. As if this situation were not at all unusual.

There was something familiar about it. In a way, it felt like old times.

Just with corsets. And a man, not a boy.

It was not like old times at all.

Good lord, she was going daft.

"Let's do this," she said firmly. It was deuced awkward but he climbed up, then she did, then he lifted her high enough so that she could swing one leg over the ledge. And then another. She held on, then let go, sliding down the stone wall and landing with a thud on her bottom.

The sound of chattering party guests reached her, and in a flash she was unlatching the door and stepping inside— holding the door open, wide open, of course, and taking great care to keep it thus.

Even as she swiftly donned her dress and James made short work of the buttons and smoothed some of the wrinkles in her gown.

"My hair," she whispered, tentatively raising one hand to the incriminating mess it had become.

"The wind. It's incredibly windy today," James lectured. Indeed. Now if only wind could explain the telltale signs she'd been on her knees.

"You should go immediately to make your speech. Don't worry about me," she told him.

"I should worry about you. But oddly enough, I fear more

for whoever encounters you," he said. She smiled, because she knew it was a compliment.

She cast a wary eye over his appearance. His hair was also disheveled. His cravat had gone limp. Dust and dirt flecked his jacket. And his breeches . . . stained at the knees and ripped quite nearly up to his backside.

Charlotte brushed off his jacket. It was the least she could do.

"Well, it has been . . ." she started, her voice trailing off.

". . . a pleasure," James said firmly. Her heart beat hard with happiness. She had missed him. And she did not want to miss him again.

Charlotte's last glimpse of the garden party—as she was swiftly and discretely hustled out by her brother and sister-in-law—was James standing before the guests delivering his speech. The wind blew, ruffling his hair and lifting the tails of his coat, exposing the unseemly rip in his breeches. Lord Hastings was horrified. The guests were aghast. Any words he said were lost in the wind.

They would say that he looked disgraceful. Charlotte thought he looked utterly dashing.

Brooke's Gentleman's Club

Later that night

"Well that went badly," James remarked to his old friend, Nathanson. There was not enough brandy. Or whiskey. Or wine. James's heart was still racing from all the narrowly averted disasters of the afternoon.

"I'm dying to know what the devil happened to you, James. And do not repeat that hogwash about saving the kitten from the tree," Nathanson implored.

In spite of himself, James grinned. When he found himself a disheveled unsightly mess standing before two hundred guests expecting a speech on architecture and the achievements of his father, James's mind went blank.

Save for one thought: *What would Charlotte do?*

Because he knew her, he knew that she would brazen through. She would concoct a story just shy of utterly unbelievable. And she would defend it until her dying breath. So he did just that.

First, he started off by offering the services of his valet and offered his present attire as recommendation. A few people in the crowd laughed.

Next, he mentioned having saved a kitten from a tree as an explanation for his disheveled appearance. After all, who could find fault with the rescue of a kitten?

Never mind that there was no kitten.

James then began speaking of his father's interest and dedication to his study. He was presently surprised to find that all those things he'd read about had somehow lodged in his brain and were available to him in his hour of need. James spoke of the folly's features and praised it for its beauty and security (that was for Charlotte).

All in all, he did not do a terrible job.

But all anyone seemed to notice was the massive hole in the backside of his breeches, revealed with every gust of wind.

It had been an unusually windy day.

"You know, I can't decide which was my favorite part,"

Nathanson remarked, grinning. "The gasp of the crowd when you stepped up to speak, looking as if you had lost a wrestling match with a rabid wild boar, or your father's grim expression when he saw the hole in your breeches."

"I'm glad someone finds humor in it," James replied. He could see the humor in all of it. His father could not. James took a long sip of his whiskey.

"How angry is he?" Nathanson asked gingerly.

"The thing to remember is that even if I had pulled it off perfectly, he still would have thought Gideon could have done better," James said. The sad fact was that Gideon could do no wrong and James could do no right.

"Ah yes, the revoltingly perfect heir and older brother, fluent in five languages—" Nathanson said dryly. They'd all been at school together. Gideon had been as smug, perfect and insufferable then as he was now.

"Seven," James corrected.

"Royal ambassador to Greece," Nathanson said, waving his hand dismissively.

"France and Germany, as well," James added, his mouth a grim line.

"With a portrait hanging in the National Gallery," Nathanson carried on.

"Two, actually." One of which was a Hastings family portrait featuring Gideon and their father in the foreground, standing tall and proud. Gideon had painted James into the background in a manner that could only be described as skulking.

Which meant he could make any manner of wisecracks about how he was skulking in the National Gallery. *James, did you call upon your Aunt Agnes? No, I was too busy skulking around the National Gallery.*

"You're right, you never had a chance," Nathanson said, shrugging. He raised his glass nevertheless and they both drank. James didn't want to say that his father's constant disappointment in him was a dead weight he carried with him. He'd long ago liberated himself from spending his life to become someone he wasn't. But he still wanted to be appreciated for who he was.

Nathanson mistook James's silence for brooding about the afternoon's disaster.

"It'll all blow over in time. Some other scandal will explode and distract everyone. Speaking of looming scandals," Nathanson said, dropping his voice and leaning in, "I heard that Lady Charlotte Brandon was seen sneaking off early in a state of utter disarray."

"Did you?" James asked, adopting a bored tone of voice and sipping his whiskey in an effort to distract from the knot forming in his gut.

"Swan Lucy saw her leaving early, escorted by the duke and duchess. Then Swan Lucy mentioned it to her friends. Lord only knows how far the story has traveled now. But it's Lady Charlotte . . ."

Nathanson didn't need to say the rest of that sentence for James to know he meant that such eccentric behavior was considered normal for her.

"Can a girl named Swan Lucy really be trusted?" James mused, leaving Nathanson to ponder that.

James drained his cup, brow furrowing. Swan Lucy gossiped about her friend—when Charlotte had been planning to set her up with a marriageable man.

His heart ached for her in that moment. Not that he would ever admit it. But the fact was that as curious and reckless and insane as Charlotte was, her heart was good. Her intentions were noble.

He could practically hear her saying, "Exactly. You're welcome."

Which meant that he was going mad. He refilled his glass and took another sip. In spite of the day's disasters and humiliations, he'd had *fun* for the first time in far too long. And he had Charlotte to thank for it.

Part Two

LADY CAPULET'S BALCONY

Hamilton House

The Informal Dining Room of the East Wing
The following morning

Charlotte would have to do something to fix the damage she had wrought. She mulled over the matter during breakfast with her brother, Brandon, and his wife, Sophie. Charlotte adored them both, especially Sophie, who had a wicked sense of humor and scandalously wrote about weddings for *The London Weekly*. Sophie had also taken on chaperone duties while Charlotte's mum visited with her sister Amelia, and her newborn twins.

Her pet fox, Penelope, sat attentively at Charlotte's feet politely begging for scraps of food. She never missed a meal.

"Charlotte, you're awfully quiet this morning," Sophie said.

"You know how your silence terrifies me," Brandon said.

He gave her one of those Serious Looks, which invited her to be honest and good and confess everything.

Charlotte developed a sudden fascination with the intricate embroidery on the tablecloth. Such detail! Such marvelous craftsmanship!

"Charlotte?" Sophie asked.

"Oh, I'm just woolgathering," Charlotte said. Then she smiled for extra effect. *Nothing to see here! Other than this stunning embroidery on the tablecloth! Has anyone considered framing this?*

"Why do I find that prospect more terrifying than reassuring?" Brandon asked dryly.

"Are you perchance thinking about the mysterious events of yesterday's garden party?" Sophie asked. Then she sipped her tea and allowed the words to hang in the air.

Charlotte dangled a piece of bacon for Penelope, who leapt up for the treat, snapping her jaws and narrowly avoiding Charlotte's fingers.

"I trust you are feeling better after fainting into a muddy bramble bush," Brandon said. She might have told him the dirt stains on her dress and her disheveled hair were the result of a slip and fall into a shrubbery. As one did.

"What a dreadful experience that must have been," Sophie said, shuddering delicately.

"Dreadful," Brandon echoed. "And curious, too, for it has not rained in a fortnight."

Stupid weather. Stupid facts. Who kept track of when it had last rained? Her brother, that's who.

"I presume the landscape had been watered for the garden party," Charlotte replied evenly. One must not let pesky details like a lack of rain get in the way of one's alibi.

Especially considering what was on the line: Marriage. To James. Who thought her a nuisance, at best, and probably still saw her as a twelve-year-old girl aiming an arrow at an apple on his head. Hardly the romantic relationship of a girl's dreams.

"How silly of me. Of course they watered the garden for the party. Particularly the bramble bushes," Brandon said. Pointedly.

"Attention to detail and nourishment of all life is such an admirable quality. I think we ought to applaud Lord Hastings for the dedication to the life in his garden," Charlotte said grandly.

She debated *actually* applauding, but Sophie cut in.

"Speaking of Lord Hastings, you would not believe what Julianna told me," Sophie said, referring to her best friend and secret gossip columnist for *The London Weekly*. "She has learned that Hastings is so livid about James's speech that he is refusing to see his own son! The family butler was instructed to turn James away on three separate occasions since yesterday's calamity."

Charlotte gasped. Penelope fortunately chose that moment to yip, though her yip was a bloodcurdling sound.

Brandon sighed in that long-suffering way of a man who is stuck with a sister who thinks it perfectly suitable to keep a pet fox in London.

"I thought his speech was fine. What I heard of it, at any rate," Charlotte added in a mumble. She had been swiftly hurried away from the party and bundled into the carriage.

"James also looked as if he had tumbled into a muddy bramble patch," Brandon remarked. "Curious, that."

"It's one of the many hazards of garden parties. They are appallingly dangerous situations," Charlotte said sagely.

"What we heard of his speech wasn't terrible. I thought his joke about his valet rather funny," Sophie said.

"He did well, though he might have practiced more," Brandon said. "Instead of tumbling into a muddy briar patch."

"I'm sure James and his father will mend this breach. After all, one cannot stay angry at family forever," Charlotte said pointedly. "Forgiveness and unconditional love is the essence of familiar relations."

"Lord Hastings has again repeated in public that James is the price he pays for his perfect son, Gideon, and that he thanks his Lord and Maker that Gideon is the heir," Sophie said, undoubtedly repeating intelligence from Julianna.

"I have heard him make similar remarks at the club," Brandon said in a quiet, disapproving voice that reminded Charlotte why she would lie down in front of a team of charging horses for him: Her brother might not approve of her behavior, but he would *always* love her and stand by her.

She wished such unconditional love for James. Her heart ached to think of him without it. She must do something. It was her fault that James's speech had been terrible and his attire a mortifying mess and thus it was her fault that his father had practically disowned him.

She must repair what she had broken.

It was the right thing to do.

"I do believe it is time for me to *walk* Penelope," Charlotte said and on cue her little fox yipped wildly and dashed to the dining-room door.

Not for the first time did Charlotte think that every lady must have an exit strategy. She personally had seven.

She removed a length of ribbons from the pocket of her dress and tied one end around Penelope's neck, thus fashioning a makeshift lead and collar for her. As they walked, Charlotte would concoct the perfect way to mend the relationship between James and his father.

"Charlotte, you are not going to meddle in the affairs of the Hastings family, are you?" Brandon asked.

"Me? Meddle?" Charlotte queried, the picture of innocence.

Sophie snorted, in a most unladylike fashion, and nearly spit out her tea.

Lady Charlotte's Bedchamber

Two ladies schemed over a pot of tea. To be precise, one lady schemed, and another sipped her tea and nibbled on freshly baked scones with strawberries and clotted cream. Charlotte's fox curled up in a little ball of red fur, resting atop the plump pile of pillows on Charlotte's feather bed. It was her favorite place.

"Harriet, I must repair the damage I have done," Charlotte said as she paced around her bedchamber. Her heart ached with the knowledge that her antics had been the lethal blow to the weakened relationship between father and son. Fixing it was the only way to soothe her conscience and repair the damage.

"How?" Harriet asked, as she idly stirred a third spoonful of sugar into her tea.

"I could write an apology—as James, of course—and send it off to *The London Weekly*. I'm sure they would publish it."

"James might not like forged documents on private matters appearing in the most popular newspaper in London," Harriet pointed out.

"You're right," Charlotte agreed, reluctantly. "This is a private family matter, and thus should be repaired in a private manner."

"I heard that Lord Hastings will not even see his son! My mother and her friends were discussing it. Apparently the family butler told James that his father was not at home, when he was in fact examining the decorative Corinthian columns in the foyer."

"That's horrible," Charlotte said. Tears stung at her eyes.

It was tremendously useful to be able to summon tears on command, and one had to practice.

"Absolutely devastating," Harriet concurred. "Too busy examining his column. Hmmph."

"So you agree that we must do something to remedy this," Charlotte said, and she resumed her pacing across the plush Aubusson carpet.

"Well . . ."

"I know!" Charlotte exclaimed whirling around. "I could write a letter to Lord Hastings. As James."

"You could do, but . . ."

"Though he will probably toss it straight into the fire without reading it," Charlotte said, frowning.

"Maybe you should *not* write a letter. To anyone. About anything. Ever." Harriet suggested.

"You're right—we should endeavor to get them in the same room together."

"Lord and Lady Capulet are hosting a ball on Thursday. Perhaps then?"

"That would be the perfect occasion. I really feel that if we all had an honest, heartfelt conversation then all will be well," Charlotte said confidently.

"We?" Harriet echoed. "*We?*"

"Hastings, James and myself," Charlotte explained.

"Why must you be there?" Harriet asked, and Charlotte stifled a feeling of peevishness. She knew she had different definitions of what was her business and what was considered other people's private personal matters.

"I must explain that what happened was not James's fault. Since Hastings will not listen to his son, perhaps he will listen to me."

"So you will admit to being compromised?" Harriet gasped. She fell back against the settee, dramatically. One had to practice such arts.

"Hastings wouldn't make anything of it. He'll be so happy to learn that James was not at fault. I think. I hope."

"But Charlotte, what if he makes you marry James?" Harriet voiced this question with the same level of horror with which she might ask *what if Lord Hastings horsewhips you? What if you are transported to Australia on a convict ship?*

"We shall cross that bridge when we come to it," Charlotte said, when in fact the truth was that James would *never* marry her, so the point was moot. She had once shot at him with an arrow. He had broken her heart with his years of silence and avoidance and his despicable taste in acquaintances. They could never be together.

She hadn't even considered James like *that*, for years.

Since 1817, to be exact. But ever since their escapades at the folly, the thought had been crossing her mind ~~every moment of every hour of every day~~ with a vexing frequency.

James . . . his blues eyes fixed upon her, really seeing her (and, frightfully, reading her mind). James . . . his voice husky as he ordered her to remove her dress and then climb a stack of crates, slip through a window and slide down a seven-foot stone wall. James . . . his fingertips brushing against the exposed skin of her back.

She shivered now just thinking about it.

He was not boring like so many gentlemen of her acquaintance. He was not boring at all.

"You often say that one should anticipate every detail and plan accordingly," Harriet said. "So you should plan what you will do if you are forced against your will to marry James."

Charlotte bit back the most startling collection of words that arose, unbidden: Oh, I wouldn't be *forced* to marry him. Not because no one would insist upon it, but because she would not fight it.

There were worse fates. Like having a man refuse to marry you after he ruined you. Which is probably what James would do. Like most men, he probably thought her too much of a bother. And she could not live with someone who felt thusly about her. Especially if she ~~fancied him~~ held him in mild regard.

"I shall declare that you were with James and me, and thus we were chaperoned. Thus, there need not be any forced marriages," Charlotte said. Thus, the problem would be solved.

"But that's not true. You were alone, quite alone, with a gentleman for three quarters of one hour. I am assured that is plenty of time to be ruined."

"How do you know that, Harriet?"

"I overheard it in the ladies' retiring room at a ball once. I had pretended to faint because I was trapped in conversation with Drawling Rawlings," Harriet explained and Charlotte nodded in absolute agreement. Lady Drawling Rawlings had been a notorious conversation monopolizer and one made every effort to avoid her. "I was taken to the ladies' retiring room, and in no rush to resume my wallflowering in the ballroom, so I feigned an epic swoon. Lady Layton and her friends thought I wasn't listening to their shocking conversation. But I was, Charlotte, *I was.*"

Charlotte sat down next to Harriet and poured herself a fresh cup of tea.

"You must tell me everything, Harriet."

And she did.

One hour later, Charlotte was much more interested in marriage and marital relations, in particular. Apparently one could be ruined in less time than it took to drink a cup of tea and this was lamentable. Allegedly, ruination could also last all night and happen again in the morning.

There was much to consider but later, in private.

"I shall just inform Lord Hastings that James and I were only together for a mere, fleeting moment and will hope that he overlooks that detail. Now, you and I must determine how to unsuspectingly lure the gentlemen into a private chamber where I shall await them to explain that they needn't be angry at each other."

"Should we just send them mysterious, unsigned notes?" Harriet suggested.

"I fear notes are too easily intercepted," Charlotte said, frowning. "Remember what happened with The Tattooed Duke."

"That was an epic disaster," Harriet said, shuddering as Charlotte cringed at the memory. That was the incident which had led to Brandon's seven-hour lecture (or so it felt) upon the imperative of minding one's own business and not meddling with fate, destiny or anything at all. It was at the end of such a brutal set down that he'd extracted her promise: *No more schemes.*

Charlotte dismissed this thought.

"We need something devious," she said. "Something that cannot be traced back to us. What do we know about James?"

"He's handsome as the devil," Harriet said quickly. Charlotte stifled a shocking and confusing flare of *jealously.* Did Harriet fancy him?

But that was her private emotion to puzzle over later.

Instead, she shrugged her shoulders and replied, "I suppose," in a casual sort of voice.

"How do you *suppose* such a thing? He is undeniably utterly handsome. His hair, his eyes, the way his breeches cling to his well-muscled thighs," Harriet said dreamily and Charlotte was aghast, but had to concede the truth. Then, peering curiously at her friend, Harriet said, "Anyone would agree."

"That is beside the point," Charlotte declared. "What else do we know of him?"

"You're the one who grew up with him," Harriet pointed out.

"We hadn't spoken for years," Charlotte said bitterly. For no reason. He stopped talking to her for no real reason. She sucked in a sharp breath because it still hurt, especially given the knowledge that they were speaking now only because of her own instigations. He had not sought her out. She so wished he would.

"Might I point out that you were locked with him in a folly for the better part of an hour," Harriet said. "If you didn't converse, Charlotte, *what did you do?*"

"We endeavored to escape because someone forgot to come with the key at the appointed time!" Charlotte took a deep breath when Harriet looked affronted. "Never mind all that. James is like all men of his ilk—"

"—Devastatingly handsome, ruthlessly charming rakes," Harriet said breathlessly with an enchanted smile and dreamy sigh.

"Yes, that. He likes drinking, wenching, wagering, pissing contests—"

"—Ravishing maidens in dark, secluded parts of the garden lit only by the light of a full moon . . ." Harriet carried on.

"Wagers!" Charlotte exclaimed.

"You said that already, Char," Harriet pointed out.

"We just need to concoct a wager that will send him to the library," Charlotte said confidently. Men never could resist a wager. Golly, this would be child's play!

"And Lord Hastings?"

"I know just the gossip that will attract him," Charlotte said, grinning wickedly.

"You have that look in your eye again, Charlotte," Harriet said. "The one that makes me nervous."

"Like I am struck by my own brilliance?"

"I was going to say maniacal," Harriet replied.

"That may very well be, Harriet. But I shall be a maniacal, brilliant young woman who will engineer a truce between two warring factions. Peace shall reign in London once again . . ."

"Are there any more biscuits?" Harriet interrupted. "All this scheming has made me quite famished."

Lady Capulet's Ball

The Eversham Motif was the newest, most au courant architectural detail ever to grace an English home, and therefore the world. Lord and Lady Capulet were the very first to incorporate the incomparable, revolutionary, stunning Eversham Motif into the construction and decoration of their London home.

Everyone who was anyone knew that. Presently, Charlotte was the only one who did. But that would soon change.

"Lady Tweetley, you must have seen it," Charlotte murmured directly into the ear of London's biggest, fastest gossip.

In a moment, Charlotte would confide in her. Harriet was stationed on the far side of the ballroom. They both watched the clock, as they timed how long it took information related to Lady Tweetley on one end of the ballroom to reach the other. It was a party game they frequently played for diversion at tedious society events.

No wonder they were not married.

"Have I seen what, my dear?" Lady Tweetley asked, inclining her head. Her hair was an unusual shade of orange, suggesting some unnatural effort, and it was incredibly frizzy.

Charlotte looked around conspiratorially, suggesting with just her gaze that the information she was about to impart was secret, confidential, scandalous and utterly salacious. Lady Tweetley actually licked her lips in anticipation.

"The Eversham Motif. It's the very latest thing in home decoration," Charlotte said.

"Stunning, isn't it? I saw it in the drawing room last Thursday. Old news!" Lady Tweetley replied. Charlotte smiled, truly smiled. Nothing amused her more than the ton's desperation to seem in the know, which meant that they often agreed to anything—especially if it was suggested by the dear sister to a duke and his fashionable duchess.

Charlotte's other favorite party game was to suggest outrageous things and see what people would agree to. Once, she had the Duchess of Richmond swearing to a correspondence with Lady Millicent Strange, who did not, in fact, exist. Nor had Lady Strange suffered her hand being bitten off by a wild boar, as Charlotte had claimed and the duchess lamented.

"Last Thursday?" Charlotte echoed. "Oh, then you haven't seen the very latest. A new Eversham Motif has been chiseled into the library this very afternoon! It's supposed to be a secret until the drawings and the secret history are revealed in an exclusive article for *The London Weekly*. Wouldn't you just die to have a peek before anyone else in London?"

"Goodness!" Lady Tweetley exclaimed, snapping open her fan and waving it quickly. "One does love to be ahead of the curve. Sneak peek! First glimpse!"

"Of course. Such a rare honor that would be for one lucky person," Charlotte said. "But do you know what is even more thrilling, in my humble opinion, that is?"

"What, dear?"

"I just love being the one to tell everyone. Sharing exciting news is just so thrilling, don't you agree?"

"Oh very much," Lady Tweetley concurred. And then she lowered her voice. "Who, pray tell, have you told, Lady Charlotte?"

"Just you, Lady Tweetley, just you," Charlotte said, smiling mischievously.

"You are such a darling girl," Lady Tweetley said, smiling and patting Charlotte absentmindedly on the arm. And then off she went, sashaying through the ballroom, bending the ear of anyone who would listen.

"Have you seen the Eversham Motif? It's the latest, the very latest, in home architecture and it is on display in the library. First Glimpse!"

Charlotte remained in her spot, watching as news of her invented architectural motif was spread around the ballroom.

And then she caught James's eye. He stood twenty paces away. Yet she saw that he raised his brow, curious and questioning, as if he knew she was up to something. That was the thing about James: He knew her. And he wasn't afraid to question her.

Everyone else foolishly fell for her schemes again and again. No one ever tried to stop her, or even better, outsmart her at her own games.

But James . . . he knew just by looking at her from halfway across the ballroom.

Three minutes after Charlotte's conversation with Lady Tweetley, Harriet arrived by her side, breathless.

"The news has officially reached the other side of the ballroom. That was fast, even for Lady Tweetley! Who knew anyone cared so much about an architectural thingamajig."

"The ton never ceases to amuse," Charlotte said, linking arms with her friend. "Onward to phase two, Harriet!"

Arm in arm they proceeded to the card room where they sought out the lamentably named Mitchell Twitchell. He was predictably found wagering more than he could afford on dreadfully bad hands of cards in a game with the nefarious, despicable pet-eater, Lord Dudley.

The two girls stood behind him and began their strategic conversation.

"I overheard the most fierce wager," Charlotte said to Harriet loudly. "I literally staggered when I heard it. And then I swooned."

"Oh? What fierce wager did you overhear? I am all agog to know. I shall perish if you do not tell me this instant," Harriet said. She dramatically draped her palm across her brow.

"It's highly confidential," Charlotte said.

"It must be immensely fascinating," Harriet replied loudly.

"A fortune is at stake! All over a one of a kind treasure," Charlotte declared.

"What's this wager you speak of?" Mitchell Twitchell cut in, pushing back from the card table and leaning back to better converse with them.

"Oh, it's the most fascinating thing, Mr. Twitchell. Lord Derby has wagered with the Earl of Sandwich that Lord

Capulet possesses the very first book from the very first edition of *The Hare Raising Adventures of George Coney*. It's a salacious memoir."

"A book? How dull."

Charlotte smiled benignly. She had anticipated that Mitchell would find a book boring. She doubted he even read his IOUs. However, James would find the book interesting, and it was James they sought. Mitchell would talk.

"Yes, well everyone is talking about it," Charlotte told him. "I am assured all the most sporting gentlemen will gather there to witness the unveiling. If I were a gambling man, I would hate myself for missing it."

"Really, how would you live with yourself if you missed it?" Harriet questioned sharply.

"I couldn't. I simply could not go on," Charlotte said gravely.

"Do you feel faint just thinking about it? I feel quite faint," Harriet rasped.

"Let us retire to the ladies' retiring room and restore ourselves with smelling salts."

In fact, they proceeded directly to the library for phase three.

In the Library

The scene in the library was just delightful. At least two dozen party guests tromped through the room, bumping into all the furniture and each other because their necks were craned as they sought the Eversham Motif.

Lady Inchbald declared it a marvel.

Lord Talleyrand bumped into an occasional table, knocking over a crystal decanter of brandy, which shattered on the parquet floor.

Lord Hastings stood lecturing a small gathering on its cultural significance.

Lord Capulet stood in the center of it all, mopping the sweat from his brow. Charlotte could tell he was torn between protecting his newly constructed and decorated library and disavowing sole possession of the single most fantastic architectural detail in the world.

Which, she did not point out, did not exist.

James sidled up to her and she felt a spark of pleasure, like the first flame from a dried leaf under a magnifying glass on a hot day. He leaned in close and murmured something only she could hear.

"I'm not quite sure what you are planning, Charlotte, but did it really require most of the party tromping through the library, much to the dismay of Lord Capulet?"

"Oh, hello there, James," she replied. "Have you come to see the settling of the wager over *The Hare Raising Adventures of George Coney?*"

Charlotte glanced to the right, where the Earl of Sandwich was combing the bookshelves in search of the elusive tome.

"The Eversham Motif, actually," he said. And she saw it—the tug of a grin. A spark of pleasure settled into a smoldering fire in her belly.

"I hope you are not disappointed," she remarked.

"To the contrary. I am surprised to find I am impressed,"

he said softly. She knew that it was a compliment; that he was impressed with her. Someone, finally, had noticed her cleverness. She was glad, deeply, that it was he.

"I thought you would be more interested in the first book of the first edition of *The Hare Raising Adventures of George Coney.*"

"I would be if such a thing existed," he said softly, tilting his head slightly. She did not want the game to end just yet.

"Oh, did they review the volume already? I hope you did not wager overmuch," she said, appearing vitally concerned for his bank accounts lest he had gambled his last farthing on the existence of a fictitious book.

"Charlotte . . ." James said warningly.

"Oh, look, Lord Hastings!" she called brightly.

"Lady Charlotte," he said in a polite, but cold greeting. He could not snub her—being so closely related to a duke, and being his longstanding neighbor in Hampshire, as she was—but it was clear he wanted to. Most likely because of the man by her side.

"I was hoping we might have a word with you," she said, and then before either gentleman could protest, she grasped their arms—lightly to the observer, but like a vise to the men—and steered them over to a private corner of the library.

The crowds served a great purpose, for the public venue prevented either gentleman from acting out. Furthermore, a mention of the Eversham Motif on the ceiling meant that all eyes were focused up, thus completely missing all sorts of scandals in their midst.

Such as two of London's feuding gentlemen in conversation, mediated by the formidable Charlotte Brandon.

"I cannot fathom what possibly we would have to talk about," Lord Hastings said icily.

James glared at them both.

"James's terrible speech was my fault," Charlotte said in a low voice. "I wanted you to know that. And to not hold it against your son."

"Charlotte . . ." James's voice was a warning, a plea . . . and it was lost to Lord Hastings's sudden lecture.

"Lady Charlotte," he began and even she shrank slightly under his withering glare. "I believe in honoring one's commitments in a prompt and dignified manner. I believe that gentlemen conduct themselves in a certain way—including, but not limited to, the attire they choose to appear in when in public. Above all, I firmly believe in minding one's own business."

"But—" James clasped her hand and squeezed. Hard.

"I shall not question your involvement in this entire matter, Lady Charlotte, nor shall I report it to your brother, His Grace. I trust you will not grant me sufficient motivation to reconsider. You are welcome."

The tears that stung Charlotte's eyes were not feigned or summoned at will. For all of her noble efforts and good intentions, Lord Hastings simply delivered a devastating set down—and he hadn't even listened to the speech she had planned! And he had used her own favorite retort against her. It was unforgivable.

No, Lord Hastings, *you* are welcome, she huffed to herself.

Lord Hastings did not even deign to acknowledge his son before stalking off. Lord Capulet finally decided that the preservation of his newly redecorated library trumped the elusive Eversham Motif and *The Hare Raising Adventures of George Coney.*

In an effort to avoid being ushered out along with the mob, James tugged Charlotte into a private window alcove.

On one side, French doors opened onto a small balcony overlooking the terrace. The thick walls—about two feet deep—formed the sides and luxurious velvet curtains draped on either side of the alcove's opening into the library.

There was room for the two of them. Just.

The only time James had seen Charlotte cry was when George Coney had died. No, that wasn't quite right. When he laughed at her for thinking to bury the beloved pet with hymns and a recitation of memories. The worst, of course, was when she had encountered Dudley. With her pet. Over an open fire.

The doctor actually sedated her with laudanum. The boys were soundly punished, and sent back to school early . . . before Charlotte had awoken.

He'd always felt shame about how he acted that day.

While he had not taken a bite, he had not tried very hard to stop Dudley, who threatened each and every day to dunk James's head in the privy. He was a bully to this day, which made the whole thing worse. James had hurt the fragile feelings of a really terrific girl to impress a bloody idiot.

And now tears were perched menacingly and he would be damned if she cried because he hadn't defended or befriended her again.

So he tugged her into the alcove so they might have some

privacy. Immediately, he regretted it. There was barely enough room for them both and it was impossible to forget that she was no longer a girl, and very, very, very much a woman. Especially as every slightest movement resulted in a complete caress.

"Charlotte you must not let him get to you," he said. "My father is an arse."

She sniffed, and blinked back the tears. He allowed a small exhalation of relief.

"He's so ungrateful! The lengths I went to in order to issue a heartfelt apology! *I invented an architectural motif for him*," she hissed.

"Upon which he lectured at length further solidifying his reputation as London's architectural expert. You are too kind," James said. She was either kind or insane; at the moment he was feeling charitably toward her for he could see the marvelous chain of events she had set in motion so that he and his father might mend their rift.

"I know that. But why doesn't he see it?" she asked, miffed.

"Because he cares only for blocks of stone, architectural whatever and Gideon," James said frankly. Beyond their alcove, the room was steadily emptying as Lord Capulet herded them out.

"Doesn't that bother you?" she asked, peering up at him with her big blue eyes. He would swear that she could read minds, and see through carefully constructed facades. No wonder so many men were terrified of her.

"Not so much anymore," James said with a shrug. It was a mild annoyance that he had reconciled himself to, like a blister that becomes a callus.

A woman's laugh punctured the silence that had fallen upon the room.

James ducked his head out and saw Lady Layton and Lord Beaverbrook stumbling into the now empty library, clinging to each other in a manner than left no question as to their intentions.

"I want to see the Eversham Motif," Lady Layton giggled.

"I'll show you my motif," Lord Beaverbrook growled. James thought he might be sick.

James also realized that unless they acted now—

Too late. Lord Beaverbrook locked the library door. And then he bent Lady Layton over the desk.

James quickly yanked the sashes holding the curtains back, and the heavy velvet drapes fell together, enclosing him and Charlotte in a dark, secluded alcove in which it was impossible for them to stand without touching each other.

"Well, this is compromising," Charlotte remarked, uttering the understatement of the nineteenth century. They were stuck together in a small, dark space with another couple making loud, adulterous love on Lord Capulet's desk.

"It we get caught," he clarified. It was their only hope. And then he prayed they would not get caught. How long could Lady Layton and Beaverbrook go at it? They just needed to wait them out and sneak out undetected. And pray no one looked for them in the meanwhile.

"What about—" Charlotte asked, inclining her head toward the amorous couple, who were now loudly declaring the pleasure that they wrought upon each other.

"If we just remain quiet, they won't notice us at all. In a moment or so, they'll be very ... distracted ... then we can make our escape," James said. If only he believed it. He had visions of being stuck here all night.

"Are they doing what I think they are doing?" She wriggled in an effort to peek out of the curtains, and in doing so brushed intimately against certain portions of James's anatomy. Part of him was thrilled with this situation.

"What do you think they're doing?" James asked her, relishing the blush that crept across her cheeks.

"Marital relations," she said solemnly.

"In a manner of speaking. Except they are not married to each other, but to other people," James said.

"I want to see," she said, grinning wickedly.

"Oh, that is nothing you should witness," he told her. "There are some things which ladies—or gentlemen—are not to see."

Lord Beaverbrook's bare arse is at the top of the list.

"That was the worst possible thing you could say, James," Charlotte said, and she writhed a little more, and he groaned. Her hands crept toward the part in the curtains . . .

He forced them closed.

"Do not make me tie your wrists with this," he said, dangling the velvet sash before her wide eyes. She bit her lip. He suspected he felt more threatened, teased and tortured than she.

"You wouldn't dare," she whispered. Strangely, he wanted to. What a sight it would be for Charlotte to be still, to be at his mercy for once.

"No one would blame me," he said. But that was a lie. If he were discovered with a *bound* female, he would have to leave town. Indefinitely.

"I want to see," she whispered again. Her curiosity would be the end of them both.

"Chess. They are playing chess," he said, his voice oddly husky.

She smiled at him, like the devil with a trick up her sleeve. Then she slid down slowly, her back against the wall, her breasts brushing against him. Quite nearly on her knees—with her mouth just inches from certain excited parts of his anatomy—she turned her head, parted the curtains and peered out.

"Chess? I think you meant chest. Yes, he has his hand on her chest," she murmured. James thought of his hands on the round swells of Charlotte's breasts, then his mouth, and the thought was tempting. Too tempting. Especially with her mouth just inches from . . .

"I can't quite . . ." Charlotte tilted her head, trying to get a better view from her impossible position. She brushed against him. He groaned softly.

"It's an advanced move in . . . backgammon," James told her. Why he felt impelled to protect the innocence of Charlotte Brandon he knew not. Especially given that he'd just been considering his hands and his mouth lavishing attention on her breasts.

"If that is backgammon then I have been playing *all wrong*," she replied, and God help him, he wanted to laugh. She slid up to stand, her body torturously caressing the length of his as she did. The thing was, he didn't think this was a deliberate scheme or a purposefully seductive maneuver.

In spite of all her dangerous and devious machinations, she was an innocent.

"Don't look anymore. You'll be ruined," he said, his voice hoarse.

"One might say I already am. For the second time," she said.

"And whose fault is that?" he questioned.

Hers. But he would be blamed for it.

"Quite beside the point, I'm sure. Now step aside sir, I couldn't *quite* see and I'd like to be shocked." She tried to inch past him. He held the curtains firmly shut. Mainly, though, to keep his hands occupied with something other than her—whether a caress or strangling, he wasn't quite sure yet.

"You want to be shocked, Charlotte?" he asked, with a lift of his brow, like a dare.

"I'll settle for amused," she said coolly.

"Will you now? He replied just as coolly, even though, by God, he suddenly wanted to take her, kiss her hard and show her shocked. Ravished. Amused.

"Shouldn't a gentleman honor a lady's wishes?" Charlotte mused. "Is that not the gentlemanly thing to do?"

"It depends upon the matter in which she wishes to be obliged. I cannot in good conscience let you look at the extremely indelicate situation in which Lady Layton and Lord Beaverbrook are engaged."

"*Extremely indelicate?*" Charlotte echoed with a stifled burst of laughter. "You sound like a dowager."

"I'll have you know, Miss Charlotte, that I am a renowned rake. No woman would mistake me for a dowager," he said, warningly.

"Why does that sound like a threat?"

"It isn't," he said firmly. But he was *this close* to proving to her thoroughly and assuredly that he was not a dowager. He was a rake and he would take his pleasure where it suited him.

Starting with her. He would kiss that impish, teasing smile right off her mouth until she was gasping his name and her lips were red and swollen from his kiss.

"Isn't it?" she asked. He thought he might have heard her mutter "pity, that" under her breath, but he was distracted by Beaverbrook loudly and vehemently invoking the Lord's name and that of his son. And Lady Layton loudly and repeatedly affirmed that yes, yes, yes, that was just right, right there.

"Goodness . . ." Charlotte murmured and a blush infused her cheeks. "We need to get out of here. I will be missed."

"They're just about done," he said. The torture was almost over. He felt something then . . . something that made him perfectly understand Charlotte's whispered "pity, that." This was a horrendous situation.

But it was fun. Certainly more fun than inane conversations in the ballroom and waltzes with insipid young girls or blatant illicit proposals from widows and married women. Given the choice, he would choose to be here, in this miniscule alcove, with the tempting and vexing Charlotte Brandon.

The realization made his heart stop in his throat.

Yes, this was *fun*.

And it could be much more fun if he were much less of a gentleman.

Besides, it was time to plot their escape, now that Lady Layton and Beaverbrook had finished. Oh wait—oh no.

"I could just take you again!" Beaverbrook cried out.

"Yes, take me! Now! Again and again and again!" Lady Layton gasped.

Charlotte met his gaze and simply said, "We could try the window," and he wasn't sure if that was the best thing or the worst thing she could have said given that he was seriously considering ravishing her.

Charlotte thought he'd been acting peevish. He must have been so annoyed to be stuck thusly with her. Plus, she knew that Harriet would be wondering about her; ditto for Sophie and Brandon. And she could not explain that she was stuck in an alcove with a known rake. It was worse than being stuck in the folly.

Here, it was physically impossible for them not to touch. She'd felt the length of him, all strong, as she slid down to peek through the curtains. Had she known . . . she would have stood still and tall, a perfect specimen of an ideal lady's posture. And then she couldn't help but feel him all over, all over again as she stood up.

Lady Layton and Lord Beaverbrook seemed to be having a marvelous time. And she, and James . . . if he was such a rake why didn't he kiss her already?!

Thus she suggested the window. An escape not just from this alcove, but from her tortured feelings. Why did she force things all the time? Why didn't he want her? What was wrong with the man?

She and James cracked open the French doors and peered out. And down. Not only was it a sheer drop from the second story, but, were they to land safely, it would be among a gathering of guests seeking air.

"Is that Swan Lucy and Mitchell Twitchell in an . . .

embrace?" she asked, somewhat intrigued and somewhat shocked. Lucy was easily identified by her atrocious coiffure, which incorporated ropes of pearls and tiny little toy boats. The theme, one presumed, was shipwreck.

"It would seem so," James murmured. His face was close to hers. The proximity was disorientating. The wondrousness of it—from the heat pooling in her belly to the slow, heated blush stealing across her skin—was so strange, so new.

"Everyone is . . ." She started to say *everyone is having passionate encounters. Except me. And I'm the one stuck in an alcove with an avowed rake!*

"Everyone is what?" James asked in a whisper.

"Nothing," Charlotte said hastily. "Do you think we can escape this way?"

"Not without breaking our necks in the process," he remarked, drawing back inside their alcove.

"What will we do?" Charlotte asked, and she wasn't entirely asking about their escape route. No, she wanted to know what they would do until they were freed.

"We will have to wait them out," he said with a shrug. Then he leaned against the opposite wall—not that it was very far. He closed his eyes, exhaled, and his lips moved ever so slightly. It was the sign of someone counting backward from ten in an attempt to rein in their wilder emotions.

People made that expression often around Charlotte. She knew it well.

"So, James, how have you been all these years?"

"All these years?"

"Until our improper extended visit in the folly, you had

not spoken to me for years," she pointed out. This may start a fight. Or a conversation, at least.

"It would have vastly interfered with my rakish pursuits, like wenching, drinking myself stupid and engaging in idiotic wagers. Besides, you hadn't spoken to me, either," he replied. She had not expected that.

"A lady does not initiate relationships with gentlemen," she said, sounding as prim as she could.

"Since when do you give a damn about ladylike behavior?" he asked, lifting his brow. And then, in a murmuring voice, he said the most devastating thing: "Don't develop a sense of propriety on me now, Char."

"I won't," she said in a whisper, which may have been the most wanton, forward thing she'd ever said. He reached out and brushed a lock of her hair away from her face. Delicate. Attentive.

His eyes had darkened and he was looking at her mouth, intently. Dear God, her knees were actually going weak.

Beaverbrook also chose that moment to invoke the name of the Lord as well. Loudly. The Good Lord did not respond then, but Lady Layton did with an appalling amount of sighs and moans and cries of "oh, please."

"I wish I were allowed rakish pursuits. Or any pursuits," Charlotte said with a sigh. If she were more experienced, this whole encounter might not be so strange and puzzling. This, coming from a girl who had engaged in more than her fair share of trouble, but never *this* kind of trouble.

"You may pursue ladylike behavior and marriage," James said. Then he gritted his teeth and nodded his head firmly. As if this were a resolution he were undertaking, not she.

"Fetch the smelling salts. I am swooning with excitement at the myriad of vast and thrilling opportunities the world affords me," Charlotte replied dryly.

"If you fainted now, I would catch you," he said softly. Her heartbeat quickened. Was James flirting with her?

"You're too kind," she demurred.

"Kindness has nothing to do with it, Charlotte." And then her knees really did go weak and, honest to God, she felt light-headed too.

The problem was that the world was not equipped for a woman like Charlotte. She was too clever, too energetic. Had she been born a man, she would have usurped the throne in at least four countries already.

Truth be told, he wouldn't put it past her to do so yet.

And he wanted to be by her side when she did.

She wasn't just his childhood comrade any longer. She was a beautiful woman with a sense of adventure, unlike all the other small-minded women he had known. Life would never be boring with Charlotte.

In the meantime, his thoughts strayed again to her breasts, swelling temptingly above her white gown that declared her an Innocent. He wanted to touch, to taste. He wanted to muss up her hair again, not because her hairpins were needed to pick a lock, but because he ran his fingers through them as he kissed her thoroughly.

Lady Layton and Beaverbrook, by the sounds of it, were thoroughly engaged in a second bout of lovemaking. He wanted to block out the noise. He wanted to be truly alone with Charlotte. And he wanted to get out of this damned alcove before his self-restraint cracked.

"Thank you for trying to mend the situation with my father and me," he said. It was important that he said it.

"Oh, it was no trouble," she replied.

"You invented an architectural motif and a book," James said. Not one to do things by halves. If she were like that in bed . . .

"A young lady must keep herself entertained," she replied and he thought of her keeping herself entertained . . . in bed . . .

"Many young ladies find embroidery and watercolors an amenable pastime," he said after an embarrassing pause in which he did not think of embroidery and watercolors at all.

"We only allow gentlemen to think that," she said, grinning wickedly. "How long do you think they will carry on?"

"Do you have someplace to be?"

"Oh, I should be out in the ballroom making myself available to suitors. Or at the very least, my presence should assure Sophie that I am not off getting into trouble."

"Which is precisely what you are doing. Instead of getting yourself courted, you are getting yourself ruined. Here. With me."

A horrid thought crossed his mind: In the eyes of the world, should they be caught, they were already ruined and destined to marry. Might as well have fun and thoroughly enjoy it. Starting with a deep first kiss and ending with their own sighs, moans and invocations of the Lord.

"Technically, I'm not ruined. We have merely conversed," Charlotte pointed out. "Also, I could claim the chaperonage of Lady Sighs Ands Moans out there."

"She's hardly providing adequate chaperonage. Anyone would agree."

"Ruination always seemed like it would be more fun than this. Stuck in a window alcove. Chattering away . . ." Did she mean that sly, coy glance? Did she bite her lip to deliberately tease him or just because? He knew her, but he didn't know her romantically. Or nakedly.

"Charlotte, you are a devil," he said slowly.

"I know," she said and she gave him that naughty smile again.

"I'm trying to be honorable. And protect you from yourself," he said through gritted teeth. Her response nearly undid him.

"What if I don't want honorable intentions or to be protected?"

"Are you sure about that?" James asked in a low murmur.

He placed a hand on either side of her, bracing himself against the wall and boxing her in. Her breath became shallow and he was glad. She did not reply.

Charlotte, speechless. Impressive. He liked her like this.

"Because I've had the devil of a time *not* ravishing you in a window alcove. With other people in the room."

As if on cue, Beaverbrook cut in.

"Oh, yes! I could make love to you . . . All! Night! Long!"

"It sounds like we have time for it," James murmured in her ear, pausing to kiss the soft hollow where her neck curved to her shoulder. He breathed her in, the inexplicable scent of her, which hit him like a drug. There was no stopping now. "Unless you want to talk."

Dear God, please do not make her want to talk. James hoped this request was not lost among the many calls to God occurring in the Capulet library this evening.

"No, no I don't want to talk," she whispered.

"Me neither," he said and it was the last thing he said for a while.

When James gently pressed his lips on her neck, Charlotte shivered as her every nerve was awakened excitedly by this novel sensation. When his lips pressed against hers, her awareness of everything else in the world ceased. She didn't hear Lady Layton or Beaverbrook, or the tick tock of the clock reminding her how long she'd been absent from the ballroom. She thought nothing of the ball, or the Eversham Motif or the hard wall against her back. But she did think of his hot, possessive kiss and the unmistakable evidence of his desire for her.

She wrapped her arms around him and arched her back, needing to feel more of him against all of her.

His mouth claimed hers for a kiss that was as tentative as it was demanding. He licked the seam of her lips. She shied away from nothing. This was trouble in its most exquisite form: something wicked that made her heart beat, something new, something Young Ladies Did Not Do, something that made her, oh yes, oh God, completely forget everything.

He tasted like champagne, like a dare, like the best sort of trouble. She nibbled on his lower lip the way he'd just done to her. His hands, oh God, his hands explored her and dared her to say no to curving around her waist, dared her to say no to caressing her breasts, dared her to forbid him not to tug down her bodice.

It should go without saying that she never said no to a dare.

Thus when he shoved her bodice out of the way, freeing her breasts, she sighed and surrendered.

And then she raised the stakes and tugged off the finely crafted Melbourne Knot his valet must have spent ... who cares how long it took to do! She was kissing James, oh wait, no ... James was ... his mouth ... her breasts ...

She was sure Young Ladies Never Did *This*. But she did. And she liked it. Oh, dear God, she loved it.

James did things with his tongue, with his mouth, with his hands that made her mind cease to function, her breaths to become gasps and her only thought to be James. Love. More.

She might have said *more*.

"You want more?" he said, low.

And then James claimed her mouth once again for another one of those devastating kisses in which time ceased to register. And then James began to tug up her skirts. She wrapped her arms around him, pulling him close and savoring the mad feeling of his hard, muscled body pressed against hers.

She caressed the planes of his chest and wished to feel his bare skin beneath her palms.

His fingers skimmed along the insanely sensitive skin inside her legs ... Very young, well, Young Ladies Absolutely Never Did This, which meant she was about to allow him such liberties because if young ladies never, then it was probably wicked good fun ...

... Oh, God, it was. His fingers found her most intimate place and she thought she'd die from the newness, strangeness and pleasure of it. But he wasn't a renowned rake for nothing, so she surrendered to his touch—light at first, in slow lazy circles as if they had all week in this alcove and not a chance in the world of being interrupted. The heat started, a spark here, then a smolder. The heat and the pressure began to spread until she too was gasping his name and that of the Lord . . .

. . . Until she nearly shattered, nearly cried out his name as the most outrageously pleasurable sensations exploded over her again and again. He caught her cries with his kiss.

She slowly came back to earth, to this alcove, and became aware that he held her close. He was hard . . . and she still wanted him. Wanted *more.*

Finally, it dawned upon them that The Loudly Amorous Couple were gone. Their cries had died down and the room was silent. James peeked out of the curtain, and she saw from the relaxation of his shoulders that the coast was clear.

"Wait here, I'll make sure no one is about," he said, stepping through the curtains and leaving her alone, breathless. She peeked through the curtains, gazing at the man who had just given her the greatest pleasure she had ever known.

Her cheeks still felt warm and pink.

Quickly she pulled the curtains shut tight with a gasp.

"Oh, hello there, Dudley," James said. Charlotte shrank back from the curtains. A burst of chattering people entered the room with the despicable Lord Dudley.

"We have come to see the Eversham Motif," Dudley said coolly. "But the door had been locked."

"Just stepped in the room myself," James said. "But I heard it was over here, in this far corner. But of an even greater interest to you might be Lord Capulet's Ming vase. I have heard that it is made of an unbreakable porcelain."

"Unbreakable you say?" one of the chattering guests queried.

"It's an ancient, secret technology. His lordship gave me leave to demonstrate it," James said, picking up the delicate vase, which featured a design of roaring blue dragons against a white background. "Gather round, everyone."

Charlotte dared to peek through the velvet curtains.

James had drawn everyone's attention to the far corner, deliberately positioning them so that their backs were to her.

She recognized the gesture as one of a true nobleman or a distressed damsel's hero. He was manipulating the situation so that she might escape with her virtue intact (or what was left of it). With the crowd's attention riveted elsewhere, she would be able to escape the alcove and join the group as if nothing had happened.

As if she hadn't been quite nearly thoroughly ravished.

As if her heart hadn't changed so that what she felt for James was so new to her. He had made her, the dangerously clever girl who deferred to no one, beg "oh please" in a voice breathless with passion, just like Lady Layton. And she had liked it.

Charlotte had always known he was the one man in London who wasn't utterly dull. She just didn't know how stimulating he could be.

James raised the Ming Vase of Unbreakable Porcelain high above his head. Every gaze was riveted.

Would he truly drop it?!

Charlotte slipped out from behind the curtain, seizing the discrete opportunity to rejoin the group that James was providing.

James let the vase drop. With force. Onto the parquet floor. It promptly shattered.

Charlotte gasped with all the rest. It was the most romantic thing she had ever witnessed. James had destroyed a priceless heirloom to protect her reputation.

As the crowd burst into a froth of exclamations and chatter, Charlotte caught James's gaze. He winked.

She fell in love.

Then she was promptly distracted by the arrival of Sophie.

"Ah, there you are Charlotte! I have been looking for you. Harriet thought you might have fainted somewhere."

"I was feeling dizzy when I came in to see the Eversham Motif. All the crowds, you see. I did faint, and luckily Lady Layton and Lord Beaverbrook stayed with me until I recovered myself," Charlotte explained, knowing they would never contradict the alibi she had just created for them.

"That is too kind of them. We must find them and thank them," Sophie said.

"Indeed. Although perhaps another time. I am feeling not quite myself," Charlotte said. Wasn't that the truth! She had just discovered the most outrageous pleasure she had ever known *and* fallen in love. Somebody fetch the smelling salts.

Hamilton House

The Drawing Room

When James called upon Charlotte the following day, he was not surprised at how swiftly and deviously she engineered a moment alone.

After a moment of polite chatter with her and Sophie, her sister-in-law and chaperone, Charlotte gasped, dramatically, apropos of nothing.

"What is it?" Sophie asked suspiciously.

"I forgot to tell you," Charlotte answered meekly with an adorably sheepish shrug of her shoulders.

"Tell me what?" Sophie asked, warily.

"The nanny wished to speak to you about the baby. I was supposed to tell you at breakfast, but it just slipped my mind. I do hope it wasn't an urgent matter," Charlotte said sounding so apologetic that James almost believed it. Almost.

"Excuse me, please," Sophie said, rushing out of the room. She paused at the doorway to admonish Charlotte to "stay out of trouble" and then she dashed off.

"There was no message from the nanny was there?" he asked.

"Of course not," she replied, sipping her tea innocently. "What brings you here, James?"

That was the question. There were two things he had come to discuss.

"I had heard you fainted at the Capulet ball. I thought I might come in to inquire about your health," he said politely. But her eyes were shining with their secret and he was sure his were as well.

"You are too kind," she replied demurely.

"How are you feeling today? I hope you are improved."

"I still feel a touch faint. Perhaps a *walk* in the fresh air and sunshine would prove beneficial to my delicate constitution," she said.

"*What the hell!?*"

There was a flash of movement and the strangest sound on the far side of the sitting room; James caught it out of the corner of his eye. He startled and his shock did not cease when his brain fully registered the reason.

"I beg your pardon?" Charlotte inquired, completely oblivious.

"What the hell is a fox doing in your drawing room?" he asked. He eyed it warily as the fox in question stalked over from the settee where it had been napping, only to sit at Charlotte's feet.

In James's world, foxes were things one hunted. They were not creatures that inhabited drawing rooms.

"Oh, that's Penelope. She would probably like a *walk* as well," Charlotte said. And then the fox uttered a noise like an unearthly combination of a dog's bark and a baby's scream. It was ghastly. "That is your second cue to inquire if my fox and I would fancy a stroll in the park with you."

"Has anyone ever told you how bossy you are?" James asked, deciding to ignore that *she kept a pet fox in the drawing room*. This was Charlotte. He should not be surprised.

"I wouldn't say that I'm bossy," Charlotte remarked thoughtfully. "I just always know what to do before anyone else does and I do not keep the information to myself."

"I don't know what to say to that," James replied. And honest to God, he did not.

"Shall I tell you?" she offered obligingly.

"Bossy . . . bossy . . ." he muttered. Could he live with that for the rest of his life? Yes, he was considering . . . that. It was one of the two things he had come to discuss with her.

"But admit it—You find me vastly preferable to one of those vapid, missish creatures that are the ideal of young, aristocratic womanhood," she said matter-of-factly.

And that was the truth of the matter. He far preferred Charlotte's bossiness to other women's missishness.

"Lead the way, Charlotte," he said. She wrapped a length of blue ribbon around the fox and, after pausing for her gloves and bonnet, they set off for a walk in Hyde Park.

James quickly discovered that with Charlotte even a mere three-block stroll through Mayfair was an event. At least three respectable matrons shrieked upon seeing a fox trotting merrily alongside a young woman, bound only by a silk ribbon.

Grown men crossed the street.

Friends and acquaintances merely waved and nodded rather than pause to converse politely.

"Penelope wards off the dullards," Charlotte stated simply, and carried on, not at all bothered that people went out of their way to avoid her.

His heart broke for her a little bit. But he also admired her brilliance. After all, he didn't want to talk to any of those boring acquaintances who had avoided them. Instead, the swarm of pedestrians parted like the Red Sea as she happily strolled along.

When they got to the park, the fox slowed her pace to stop and sniff every blade of grass, shrubbery and pebble.

"I'm afraid I have bad news," he told Charlotte frankly.

"Ooh," she gasped, and her eyes widened.

"Why are you excited by that?"

"I take bad news as a challenge," she replied with a shrug, which gave him pause.

"Anyway," James said, "Dudley has been mentioning a curious thing he spied at the Capulet ball. He was part of the later tour of the Eversham Motif, as you'll recall. He was also not distracted by my breaking a priceless vase from the Ming Dynasty."

"Dudley, that loathsome pet-eating cork brain, is usually not interested in anything but himself. I cannot imagine what he saw. It should go without saying that I have an incredibly active imagination."

"He claims to have seen a particular young lady emerge from a hiding spot behind the curtains," James said. Some of the irritation he felt about the situation seeped into his voice. He wanted Charlotte, but not because the Despicable Dudley was spreading damaging rumors that would force his hand.

"Yes, I had gone to get a spot of fresh air after my fainting spell. Sometimes, smelling salts are just not sufficient," Charlotte replied, not at all bothered because she had what she *assumed* was a perfectly good reason and alibi. Perhaps it was. But Dudley was despicable. He was capable of evil.

James stopped and tugged Charlotte's wrist so she faced him.

"Charlotte, we might have been seen," he said urgently. Did she not realize the implications of that?

She sighed impatiently.

"James. Dudley is a notorious bounder whom nobody likes. Also, I put it about that Lady Layton and Lord Beaverbrook were with me as I had fainted in the library. You and I both know that they will support that story with their last dying breath."

It was his turn to sigh impatiently. She just didn't realize what he was getting at, did she? The "M" word burned on his tongue.

If necessity wouldn't compel her, he would have to resort to revealing his feelings, which were, at present: *I am in equal measures enamored and terrified of you. But enamored is winning.*

"Well, well. Speak of the devil," Charlotte said, glancing at someone past his shoulder. She called out: "Hello Lady Layton! Lord Layton!"

James groaned. Did Charlotte really just call her over—with her cuckolded husband? He had planned a romantic walk in the park and now he would have to politely chatter with a woman from whom he'd heard every panting breath and call to God during an adulterous romp. Perhaps Charlotte wasn't quite *fun* all the time, but she certainly was never dull.

"Lady Brandon. I hope you are recovering nicely," Lady Layton said kindly. It seemed Charlotte's rumor had reached her.

"Indeed. I cannot thank you enough for your tending to me. I don't know what I would have done had you not availed yourself to come to my aid," Charlotte said, smiling sweetly. Lady Layton bit her lip, obviously keen to understand *why* she had been dragged into this ridiculous tale. Yet it was impossible with her husband standing on.

"Very kind of you, dear," Lord Layton mumbled and patted his wife absentmindedly on her arm. He was old enough to be her father. James saw the romp in the library in a new light.

"It was my pleasure," Lady Layton replied graciously.

"And what a pleasure it was," Charlotte said sweetly, which caused Lady Layton to redden and James to cough.

"I say, is that a dog?" Lord Layton inquired.

"It's a fox. My pet fox," Charlotte replied.

"Is it friendly?" Lady Layton asked, though she held herself at a distance.

"Are you *friendly*, Penelope?" Charlotte inquired of the animal. On cue, Penelope growled and gave another one of those wounded dog, baby scream barks.

Both Lord and Lady Layton visibly shuddered and bid their farewells.

"I trained her to do that," Charlotte explained after they had left.

"Let me guess: You stumbled upon her, injured and alone in the forest as dusk was settling," James said, revealing his startling insight into the inner workings of Charlotte's mind. "Instead of letting nature take its course you brought her home, swaddled in your finest shawl, and personally tended to her and tamed her."

It should be noted that Charlotte did not contradict a word. Not one word.

"You should have seen her, James. I found her, wounded as if a hawk had caught then released her. She was so lonely on my little patch of land," Charlotte said, referring to the ten crucial acres of land that were part of her dowry. They comprised the only accessible part of the Avonlea River which went through their county . . . and happened to be smack in the middle of the Duke of Brandon's holdings and James's father's estate.

For the first time, James paused to question why Brandon

had added that portion to her dowry. Did he mean for her to marry Gideon? It was the only logical explanation. His father would be damn pleased if it became a part of the Hastings holdings.

"I could not leave her to her fate and let Nature take her course," Charlotte said, affectionately patting the creature on its head.

"Bossy . . . bossy . . ." he murmured again. "Lady Charlotte Brandon, who knows better than Nature Herself."

That was the woman he was thinking of marrying.

He ought to speak to her brother.

Or to a doctor.

Or the lady herself.

"Charlotte," he said in his most devastatingly rakish voice. He paused in his walking and clasped her hand in his, turning her to face him.

"James," she replied in a matching tone.

He searched her blue eyes, seeking a hint of her feelings. Was it mad of him to consider making her his wife? He didn't think so, because he thought he might just be the only man for her. The question was: Did she think the same?

He knew his days with her would be spent in a constant state of anticipation. Nights with her would give deep satisfaction to them both. With Charlotte, he would never be bored. With him, she wouldn't be stifled.

"Charlotte," he said again because he didn't know where to begin. It didn't seem she would marry him out of a sense of propriety.

It would have to be for love.

He didn't know the words for asking about that.

"Charlotte."

"James," she repeated. He detected mirth in her eyes. And then panic. "Penelope!"

The fox had apparently spied a squirrel, and apparently decided it would like to pursue that squirrel.

Charlotte pursued her pet fox.

James pursued Charlotte—but quickly overtook her thanks to his superior masculine strength and speed (and lack of skirts to tangle around his ankles). He shifted his sights to that damned fox, knowing that recapturing the animal would endear him to Charlotte forever.

Ah, courtship.

James reconsidered this method of courtship when he had to chase the fox through a thicket of shrubs and other brush, an irritating amount that bore thorns.

What ever happened to flowers? Or poetry?

Where the devil was a pack of bloodthirsty hounds when one needed them?

"Penelope!" Charlotte yelled. "James!"

He spied Penelope—standing possessively over the squirrel. When she saw him advancing upon her she emitted a low growl.

He dared to stalk closer.

What a man did for love, he thought with a sigh.

"It's all right, Penelope, I'm friendly," he said. With that, she growled again and uttered that horrid shriekish bark. Then she began wolfing down her prize as he advanced.

When he was just a few paces away, the fox picked up its quarry and dashed off. James followed, to the sound of Charlotte tearing through the brush after him. He glanced over his shoulder, seeing her cheeks flushed with the exertion, her eyes bright and determined, her hair tumbling around her shoulders, her dress torn and muddied at the hem.

She was breathtaking.

But he could not dwell on that now. Not when Penelope had taken to the Serpentine.

When he awoke this morning, James did not anticipate that he would discover just how well foxes could swim.

Penelope ran straight for the Serpentine; James followed her in up to his Hessians until it became clear the damn fox would swim across the river.

The swans were not amused.

They cried and flapped their great wings, crowding toward the shore.

Did he mention the hysterical fits occurring all around the park as this ensued? Today would have been an excellent day to be a park vendor offering smelling salts.

Thoughts aside, James saw Penelope heading toward the middle of lake.

He also, fortuitously, spied a rowboat idling by the shore.

"Charlotte, hurry," he called. They clambered about the rowboat and he set off, rowing hard and fast and ignoring the burning in his arms and the tightness in his chest.

With a few quick strokes, they were able to catch up to the maddening creature. Charlotte reached in and picked up the fox by the scruff of her neck.

"Naughty fox!" she admonished. The animal did not seem to care in the slightest. In fact, it distinctly appeared to be smiling as if to say, "Wasn't that a rollicking good time!"

Charlotte hugged the sodden creature close to her, obviously not caring one whit for her dress, which was now damp and clingingly temptingly to her curves, and did nothing to help him catch his breath.

"This is so romantic," Charlotte said, dreamy eyed and with a seductive smile.

He begged to differ—that was his first response. But then James looked at Char's happy, smiling face and attempted to see the events through her starry eyes.

A gentleman taking a lady for a scenic stroll through the park and rowing her on a boat across the Serpentine was indeed romantic.

They had enjoyed an adventure, which ended happily.

Yes, life with Charlotte as his bride would never be dull and he did not want to live a tedious life. He wasn't sure, but she would probably say yes.

One thing was certainly clear: He couldn't do anything so pedestrian as simply *ask* if she wished to marry him.

No, he would have to create a scene, develop a scheme . . . Thanks to Penelope, he had an idea . . .

"Why are you grinning like that?" she asked.

"I am happy, Charlotte. It's a lovely day. We have had an adventure. Your pet is safe. The sun is shining, the birds are singing . . ."

"I know that smile. And that wicked gleam in your eye. It's how I look when I've thought up a delicious scheme," she said, leveling him with a gaze that was a prelude to an interrogation. She had *no* idea what would be in store for her.

Part Three

THE WEST DRAWING ROOM ... OR THE EAST?

Mulligan's Ribbon Shoppe

Bond Street

"Harriet, remind me: Why are we here?" Charlotte asked, utterly perplexed as to why Harriet urgently needed to select a hair ribbon and why Charlotte's presence was necessary for the endeavor.

"I am trying new colors to see which suit me. I'm starting with hair ribbons before ordering an entire new wardrobe," Harriet explained. She selected a wide salmon-colored satin ribbon and held it up to her hair.

"No," Charlotte said.

"Thank you," Harriet replied, and she moved to examine other ribbons in a dizzying array of colors and textures.

"I see why you brought me," Charlotte murmured. "It's just as well, I need a new ribbon for Penelope."

"I heard she caused quite the scene. Actually, I heard *James* caused quite the scene."

"No," Charlotte said. "Pea green does not suit you."

"Are you avoiding the question, Charlotte?" Harriet gasped, delighted with her discovery of a Sensitive Topic.

"Should I get another blue silk ribbon for Penelope?" Charlotte mused. "Or perhaps this forest green velvet?"

"You fancy him," Harriet declared, gleefully. This had never happened before.

"I—" The strangest thing happened: Charlotte opened her mouth and found no words waiting. She must be ill.

"And you don't deny it!" Harriet now clapped her hands together in delight.

"I fail to see why this is amusing," she muttered. My God, there was something wrong with her. Speechlessness. Sense of humor failure. She was probably dying.

"I fail to see why *you do not* see that this is amusing," Harriet exclaimed loudly, thus involving the entire ribbon shop in Charlotte's business. "You fancy a gentleman! Finally!"

"Well he's the only one with a modicum of intelligence," Charlotte replied, which was as close as she could get to revealing the truth, which was that YES SHE FANCIED HIM.

"And he's *so* handsome," Harriet said dreamily, idly stroking her hands along a blue satin ribbon that reminded Charlotte of the exact shade of James's eyes.

"Tolerable, I suppose," Charlotte said with an indifferent shrug, even though she had barely slept since their afternoon in the folly and their evening in the alcove. Instead, she entertained the most wicked thoughts that definitely turned upon his breathtaking handsomeness.

His blue eyes, like the sky after a storm. His mouth, so sensual and soft against her own. His broad, muscled chest that put most men to shame. That sleek scar gracing his left cheek demonstrating either his idiocy or his trust in her.

Harriet peered at her closely. She obviously had a question to ask. Charlotte developed a sudden fascination with a puce grosgrain ribbon.

Don't say it. Don't say it. Don't say it.

"Do you think he fancies you back?" Harriet asked. Curses. *She said it.*

"I don't know," Charlotte said darkly. Of course there was evidence to support that James did, indeed, fancy her—she certainly didn't nearly ravish herself in that alcove—there was also the regrettable fact that their nearly every interaction was a scheme engineered by herself.

There was nothing she loved more than being in control. Which is why it was deuced strange she longed for James to sweep her off her feet.

Hamilton House

The Duke's Study

"You want to marry Charlotte," the Duke of Brandon repeated flatly. For the third time.

"Yes," James said confidently. For the third time.

"You want to marry my sister, Charlotte, who faints at

will, never met a wild animal she didn't want to keep as a pet and is far too clever for her own good."

"Yes, the very one," James said. In his head he corrected the duke's description: who possessed many talents, who had a large, loving heart, who was far more clever than any other woman. Charlotte, whom he adored and with whom he would never be bored.

"Brave man," the duke muttered. He nodded approvingly when he saw James's expression darken.

"She and I suit," James said simply. He hadn't intended to marry. He hadn't intended to develop feelings for a woman, and he certainly hadn't planned on falling in love. But then Charlotte happened.

Just like that day years ago, when he had no intention of befriending the impish *girl* neighbor. But she promised the wildest adventures that were too damn fun to resist.

The adventures she hinted at now were far more wicked, but just as wild, just as exhilarating.

He wanted Charlotte to keep happening to him.

He didn't want her to be with any other man because she wouldn't be happy with any other man. Charlotte's happiness was paramount.

"We are both aware that my permission is irrelevant in this matter. You must ask the lady herself. For what it's worth, I do approve," the duke said.

"Thank you, Your Grace," James said and he allowed a small exhalation of relief. The blessing of Charlotte's family mattered.

"Shall we call her in and you can ask her yourself?" Brandon offered, as he poured two glasses of brandy.

"Actually, I have arranged for her to be elsewhere today. She is currently investigating hair ribbons with Miss Harriet Dawkins," James replied.

The duke lifted his eyebrow, intrigued. James explained.

"Were I to call upon you with Charlotte at home, it would not escape her notice. And the fact of the matter is that, given the lady in question, I cannot simply propose. I must also do something dramatic. I must also give Charlotte a taste of her own medicine."

"She will appreciate that," the duke said with a smile, handing James a glass of brandy.

"I have a scheme in mind," James said. "I just need your help . . ."

The duchess was called in. A few servants were consulted and missives dispatched. By the time Charlotte returned home the scheme was in progress.

Lady Charlotte's Bedchamber

Four days later

For the third time, Charlotte crossed the room to shut her bedchamber door. Something had gone wrong with the knob or the lock or what-have-you and it popped open at the most inconvenient times, such as when two ladies were discussing a particular gentleman.

"Harriet, I'm sure James was about to say something momentous," Charlotte said broodingly to her friend. As per usual, they were lolling about with periodicals, a pot of tea and a plate of cakes, scones and biscuits. Outside, rain lashed at the windows. The weather suited her mood.

"What do you think he was about to say?" Harriet asked as she idly flipped through an issue of *La Belle Assemblée*.

"I don't know," Charlotte said darkly. She hated not knowing things. "There are really only three momentous things a man would say to a woman."

"A marriage proposal. A confession of love. What's the third?" Harriet asked.

"That he's leaving the country," Charlotte explained. She hoped it wasn't true. She hoped it *was* true and that he would whisk her along with him and together they would travel the world and have all sorts of romantic adventures.

"Leaving the country? Do you really think so?" Harriet asked, her skepticism obvious.

"Or he might have a horrid, terminal illness," Charlotte said darkly. That was the other possibility and she ~~feared life would not be worth living without James~~ did not care for it.

"I wouldn't worry about that. He seems to be the picture of health and vitality," Harriet remarked. "He's so strong, and golden."

Both ladies fell silent pondering James's sun-browned skin and the golden strands of his hair. Charlotte indulged in memories of the warmth of his skin, the taste of his lips.

The door popped open again. Charlotte sighed, crossed the room and shut it once more.

"Perhaps he was about to confess to committing a horrendous crime and he needs my

assistance in convincing a jury of his innocence," Charlotte said dramatically.

"You would be good at that," Harriet said diplomatically. Charlotte fantasized about a world in which she could be a defender of justice and make grand speeches. *Or* she could disguise herself as a man and procure a legal degree, obtain a position ... she pictured herself in gentleman's dress, striding across the courtroom and addressing a jury and interrogating witnesses while James's fate hung in the balance.

"What do you think he did? Murder? Highway robbery?" Charlotte wondered, twirling a lock of hair around her finger. She hoped it was highway robbery. She could just see him in a black mask, atop a black stallion, calling out *Stand and deliver* to carriages full of passengers all at his mercy, in the dead of a moonless night ...

"Charlotte!"

"What?"

"He didn't commit a crime," Harriet said, exasperated.

"How do you know that?" Charlotte asked, eyes narrowed, her suspicions raised.

"One just assumes the best in others ... one would think something else a more plausible possibility," Harriet said, stammering slightly. A blush crept into her cheeks.

"One would think one's friend knows something," Charlotte said slowly, her focused gaze never wavering. Harriet smoothed her skirts.

"One would think it was silly to think one's friend knows anything of the heart and mind of a gentleman with whom she is not acquainted," Harriet replied.

"The fact remains that he was certainly about to say something of great importance the other day in the park. It goes without saying that I should like to know. It also goes without saying I must engineer a meeting thus providing him opportunity."

"Why don't you write him a letter?" Harriet suggested. Even though just last week she had said Charlotte should never write another letter again, to anyone, ever.

"Dear James, I thought you might have been about to say something of tremendous importance—perhaps confessing your love for me, or confessing to a horrific crime. Do let me know. Curiously yours, Charlotte."

"It isn't every day one receives a letter like that," Harriet said. Wasn't that the truth! The post would be so much more interesting if one did. But Charlotte would not send him a letter. She wanted to see his face, with his blue eyes and that slanting scar. She wanted to hear his voice say whatever it was he'd been about to say. She wanted to feel his caress, his lips, his . . .

"I should like to see him. Alone."

"Charlotte . . ." Harriet warned. "You had quite a narrow escape at the Hastings garden party. And an even narrower escape at the Capulet ball. Do you not think your luck might run out?"

"I have plans. Not luck," Charlotte replied. She knew just the way in which to secure his undivided attention.

"Are you sure? Do you really want to risk it?" Harriet questioned nervously. Again.

"Why wouldn't I want to take the risk, Harriet Dawkins?"

"No reason . . ." her friend said meekly.

"Never mind that. I have the perfect plan," Charlotte announced.

Hamilton House

The Foyer
A few days later

The duke and duchess of Hamilton and Brandon were hosting a ball in their home to celebrate . . . well, Charlotte wasn't quite clear on the occasion for the event, and she didn't quite care. James had been invited.

More important, James had replied that *yes* he would attend. She knew this because she had personally intercepted and perused every reply that had made it into Hamilton House.

She had to do something while waiting for him to call.

That was, besides *despise* the rule that IT WAS NOT DONE for ladies to visit gentlemen.

So she read other people's mail, naturally. While James did not visit. Or write. Or in any way indicate his awareness that she existed in the world.

Logic or madness—one of the two—compelled her to recognize two facts. She had hoped he had something important to say that day. In fact, she hoped it had been a marriage proposal.

That a proposal was not issued, nor did he even pop in to chat about the weather for just a few moments, sent Charlotte spiraling to the depths of despair.

Tonight, however . . .

Tonight she would Take Action. While she usually abhorred standing in the receiving line with Brandon and Sophie, tonight it served to her advantage.

At 8:17 James arrived, looking devastatingly handsome in the stark black of his evening dress. His hair was brushed back, accentuating that scar which slanted across his cheek, drawing her gaze down, down, down to his sensuous mouth.

Charlotte stared. And paid no attention to Lady Layton's polite chatter with Sophie, though something struck her as unusual.

". . . what a coup that the author George Coney shall be in attendance tonight . . ."

Very well, that caught Charlotte's attention. It was impossible that Lady Layton had heard of George Coney because 1) George Coney did not exist and 2) it was highly unlikely she had heard about the wager at the Capulet ball and 3) the book that was the subject of the wager, like its author, did not exist.

She must be turning into one of those idiotic misses who lost brain matter in the presence of handsome men with devastating kisses, exquisitely torturous caresses and rakish smiles that made a girl weak in the knees.

Dear Lord God Above. She wanted to slap herself. But she really wanted to be swept into his embrace as his mouth crashed down upon hers for a scorching kiss. . .

"Good evening, Charlotte," James murmured, clasping her hand.

"Hello, James," she managed to reply. Her heart was beating wildly. Her thoughts were scattered wildly and she was afraid she might be blushing.

"You look fine this evening," he murmured.

"Thank you," she said, doing her best to sound demure when in fact her heart was skipping beats. He thought her pretty!

And then, oh then, James's gaze locked with hers and she ceased to notice the throngs of peers and peeresses, the music from the orchestra . . . everything went away but James. She tried to read all the unspoken thoughts and secret desires that supposedly lurked in one's gaze but she only concluded that she *wanted* him. And wanted him alone.

"Well, I shall see you later this evening, Charlotte," he murmured, squeezing her hand affectionately. Then he smiled. Then he winked. *Winked!*

"Wait—" She reached out impulsively and clasped his hand. "I have saved the fourth waltz for you."

It was immensely forward to say such a thing. But she had to speak with him and a waltz ensured at least four minutes of conversation in which neither party could flee.

There was also the small fact that she simply wanted to waltz with him.

"I shall look forward to it," he replied, not at all chastising her for such a brazen, unladylike order. That was why he was the man for her.

Hamilton House, the Ballroom

Specifically, Behind a Pillar

James thought Charlotte looked beautiful tonight. Haughty, but vulnerable. Tortured but determined. Distracted. She probably suspected that a scheme was in the works—one insti-gated by someone else for a change. Namely, by him. It wasn't every night that a man proposed and when a man was proposing to Charlotte not just any display of romance would do. No, one must have a touch of genius, be a bit devious . . .

If Charlotte hadn't suspected a scheme, she was about to.

James watched from his discrete vantage point behind the pillar as Lady Tweetley approached, armed with information that he had supplied to Lady Roxbury who had passed it along to the necessary gossips.

"Charlotte! Have you heard? George Coney is here! Tonight!" Lady Tweetley tittered before flitting off to spread this impossible news to each and every guest in attendance tonight.

"That is impossible," Charlotte said flatly. James grinned.

"Is it?" Harriet mused. James's smile vanished. It had been tricky involving Harriet for he worried how she would hold up under the strain of keeping secrets from Charlotte. But in the end, it had been essential to his plan. Someone had to make sure that Charlotte was escorted to *the west* drawing room while guests all shuffled off to *the east* drawing room.

"Of course it's impossible. You know as well as I do that George Coney doesn't exist," Charlotte said matter-of-factly. She twirled a lock of hair around her finger and he could practically see the machinery in her brain working.

The point of the gossip was for Charlotte to anticipate something. Anticipation was key.

However, there was also the problem of Harriet's nerves fraying under the pressure of Charlotte's ruthless and relentless logic.

"Perhaps there is an impersonator!" Harriet burst out.

Charlotte's expression was skeptical. And then the two girls were interrupted by the arrival of Lady Talleyrand and Lady Inchbald.

"Lady Charlotte! Perhaps you can help us. We are so keen to hear George Coney read from his book, *The Hare Raising Adventures of George Coney*. Where might we find the library?"

"Oh, no," interrupted Lord Derby. "He's reading in the east drawing room."

"It was in one of the drawing rooms, I think," Lady Inchbald said.

"No, the library!" yet another guest interrupted.

"Was it in the west drawing room or the east drawing room?" Lady Talleyrand mused. "It was one of the two. Or perhaps the north. I just cannot recall."

James didn't give a damn where these people went at midnight when George Coney was expected to "read." However, it was above all absolutely essential and imperative that Charlotte be in the west drawing room at midnight and that no one else be present.

Harriet, poor Harriet. It was her job to ensure just that.

To assist herself in that endeavor, she had written *west drawing room* on her palm. He had watched her do it.

James now watched her surreptitiously attempt to remove her glove so that she might discretely glance at the answer written on her hand and direct the throngs accordingly.

Charlotte glanced around her, absorbing the information.

James feared his carefully, well laid plans were unraveling by the second. It was deuced hot in this ballroom. Was this tension what Charlotte felt all the time since she was scheming nearly all the time?

"Well what is the worst that could happen if we go to the west drawing room and not the east one?" Lady Talleyrand asked with a piercing laugh.

Disaster, James thought. He tugged at his cravat, which had been tied awfully tight this evening.

"We shall miss a portion of the reading!" Lady Inchbald lamented.

"It's in the library," Lord Derby insisted.

George Coney doesn't even exist, James thought to himself. He was sure Charlotte was thinking the same. He glanced at Charlotte—her brow was furrowed and she was furiously thinking, he could tell.

Harriet succeeded in removing her glove.

"Perhaps you should confer with the duchess," Charlotte suggested. "Do let me know what she tells you. I would also perish if I were to miss this reading."

"We shall do just that. I should hate to miss it," Lady Talleyrand said.

"Indeed I am dying to hear from the book that is sold out in bookstores all over London! Not a copy to be had! I'm surprised you haven't heard of it Charlotte," Lady Inchbald added.

Charlotte was biting down on her lower lip. Her cheeks were flushed and her eyes were bright. One could practically see the wheels turning and the steam rising. It was clear to him that she was completely vexed by all the nonsense.

Was it wrong he thought her adorable in that moment?

"Harriet, do you know anything about this?" Charlotte asked in a remarkably calm voice after the bothersome guests had departed in search of the duchess.

"About what?" Harriet asked. She blinked her eyes for effect.

"*Harriet* . . ."

"I am parched, utterly parched," Harriet declared. Without further ado she strode determinedly toward the lemonade table—unwittingly dropping her glove where it was promptly trampled underfoot on the ballroom floor.

The Waltz

In times of uncertainty, ambiguity and chaos, Charlotte—like her dear brother—resorted to facts, and the facts were thus:

> George Coney did not exist. Certainly not in human form. Once upon a time George Coney existed as a beloved pet rabbit, who met an untimely demise.

> While gossip did have a way of getting twisted, contorted and badgered into new *on dits*, passed around on good authority, in the strictest confidence, Charlotte did not think mention of George Coney's reading at midnight was the result of people's idle chatter regarding her invented author and book at the Capulet ball Thursday last. Because . . .

> Charlotte had a sixth sense for sniffing out plots, schemes, mischief and trouble of all kinds. Tonight, she detected a scheme.

> Charlotte, it should be noted, was the grand master architect of schemes. She was not an unwitting pawn. However, tonight she suspected she was indeed an unwitting pawn!

Such were her thoughts when James approached her . . . in addition to thoughts that were utterly unladylike and completely wanton and had little to do with rumors and secret, nefarious plots and more to do with the removal of his attire.

"I believe you promised me this waltz," James said, ever the gentleman. Though she might have detected a distinctly ungentlemanly gleam in his eye. For the first time she understood the saying "butterflies in one's stomach."

He held out his hand and she placed her palm in his. Then he whisked her into his arms and swept her onto the floor, in the crush of dozens of other waltzing couples. They spun and whirled around the ballroom in perfect time with the music.

"How are you enjoying your evening?" James asked with a polite smile. She was sure he was hiding something.

"It's far more interesting than I had anticipated," Charlotte replied, hoping to convey *I know something is in the works so you might as well just tell me. Everything.*

"What good fortune," he said benignly.

She tried again.

"Like most of the people here, I am all agog for the reading of George Coney's book, *The Hare Raising Adventures of George Coney.* I imagine you must be as well?"

"You look pretty tonight," James said. Her mind went blank.

"Thank you," she replied, smiling. And then she scowled as her wits returned to her. "Also, you are avoiding the question."

"Your eyes are so blue. Like sapphires," James murmured.

"My heart is aflutter," Charlotte remarked dryly, though it certainly did feel as if her heart was aflutter. No gentleman had ever complimented her eyes before, unless to remark that she had a wicked, dangerous, maniacal gleam which she did not think was intended as a compliment though she took it as such nevertheless.

Sapphires, though. That was something.

"In spite of my fluttering heart, my suspicions are still raised," Charlotte said.

"Your mouth. I want to taste you, Charlotte," James leaned in close as he said this, so close that he could whisper it in her ear. She thought *Kiss me*. She thought *Taste me*. She thought . . .

"You are up to something. What is it?" Charlotte asked, unable to master subtly or discretion.

"Your intelligence is—" James began and she cut him off before he could finish that sentence.

"Vast. Deep. Sharp, all-encompassing," she said as he grinned. "What are you not telling me?"

"And your tenacity! 'Tis that of a terrier," James said and when her mouth dropped open in shock he hastily added, "I mean that as the highest compliment."

Charlotte loved sparring. But she hated not knowing. And she did have the tenacity of a terrier.

"You were going to say something," she said. And then she gave him her most dazzling smile to compel him into sharing his secrets.

"And the rest of you Charlotte . . . You are truly sublime," he said. The modicum of her brain that was still functioning processed this unparalleled compliment. Sublime: excellence and beauty inspiring awe. Also, so awe-inspiring as to be both magnificent and terrifying.

This was a good compliment in her book.

Her grip on him tightened. She was afraid to speak, for fear that she would confess to loving him, and to being weak-kneed with lust and delirious with desire for him.

"Oh," she said in a manner half-spoken, half-sighed. And then, "Oh, no."

They stepped quickly in three-quarter time, and James whirled them around so that he might see why she had said "Oh, no" in a very grave voice.

"Oh my God," James said. His sun-kissed skin paled.

Charlotte did her best to lead them into another turn so she could confirm that unfathomable sight.

"Is that—?" she gasped. Of all the things she had ever seen at a London ball, this was new. This was novel. She had suspected a scheme, but this was entirely unexpected.

"It is," James said, his sensuous mouth set in a grim line.

And then all hell broke loose.

In hindsight, perhaps the rabbit hadn't been the best idea. In theory, there had been a certain poetry to the gesture of gifting Charlotte with a new pet rabbit, which he took the liberty of naming George Coney the Second.

He and Charlotte had first bonded over poor, rescued George Coney the First. Their childhood friendship had ended over him. Now George Coney the Second could symbolize a new start—the start of their future together as husband and wife.

He had searched high and low in London for the perfect warm bundle of soft brown fur, shiny black eyes and velvety floppy ears.

He had left it in a wicker basket with a lid in the west drawing room. He had shut the door. Or so he had thought.

And yet, now George Coney was hopping madly across the ballroom, leaving a swath of devastation in her wake.

Yes, *her.*

Only Charlotte would give her female rabbit a man's name.

Women leapt aside, stumbling into each other as their legs tangled in their voluminous flounced skirts. Lady Talleyrand shrieked and jumped backward, effectively launching herself at Lady Inchbald, who staggered under the sudden onslaught of weight and crashed upon a footman bearing a tray of champagne flutes.

There was a terrific clatter as a dozen crystal glasses shattered upon the floor. It stole the crowd's attention for just a second before all eyes once again returned to George Coney as she merrily hopped across the parquet floor.

For a second she paused. Her little black nose started twitching and sniffing at a vigorous pace. Her long and floppy ears were pressed back against her head. James could have sworn the rabbit's eyes even widened, as if in alarm.

As if . . .

Oh bloody hell. The rabbit was definitely a bad idea.

Penelope had not been invited to join the festivities, of course, and yet she had just strolled into the ballroom.

That's when the screaming began.

It was just a *fox.* Just the sweetest, bushy-tailed, sly-eyed creature that ever stalked a rabbit in a ballroom. Honestly, the haute ton was simply awash with delicate constitutions. Out of the corner of her eye, Charlotte saw at least three women and one man swoon into the arms of their companions.

Penelope was in full huntress mode. She slinked around

bodies as if they were nothing more than trees, and leapt over fainting bodies as if they were merely fallen logs.

"Who invited her?" James muttered.

"Penelope! Come here this instant," Charlotte said.

The fox ignored her. Ignored everything except for the rabbit.

On the far side of the ballroom, the foolish rabbit stood frozen as lords and ladies bustled around it, attempting to flee the fox who was slowly, torturously stalking its prey.

Charlotte presumed that the fox had escaped—curses to her broken door!—and must have followed the scent of the rabbit. That begged the question: *Why was there a rabbit in the house?*

"Come here, Penelope," Charlotte implored. But the fox continued its hunt, oblivious to the swarms of people bumping and bustling and generally falling all over themselves in an effort to get back and who hampered Charlotte's progress in the process.

Except for one: the despicable, previously pet-eating Lord Dudley.

While most of the guests had simply made every effort to avoid the wild animal in their midst, Lord Dudley removed a pistol from his jacket.

A hush fell over the ballroom.

"No," Charlotte said in a strangled voice.

Dudley leveled the pistol at the fox, who seemed to sense the danger in the situation. Her eyes, large, glossy and black, found Charlotte, and settled there, imploring her mistress for protection. For love. For life.

Charlotte stomped forward and placed herself directly between Lord Dudley's pistol and her beloved pet fox.

"Charlotte!" At least seven different voices called her name in alarm, all from varying points in the ballroom. Well, she may be all kinds of trouble but she defended the defenseless! She protected the innocent! She loved fiercely and steadfastly.

"Lord Dudley, I'm quite sure it's an egregious breach of etiquette to shoot the beloved pet of your hostess," Charlotte declared loudly.

Lord Dudley burst out laughing.

Charlotte eyed his pistol, and considered lunging for it, and then bashing him over the head with it. Repeatedly.

He might laugh now . . .

"I don't understand why you keep killing my pets, Lord Dudley," Charlotte said, summoning tears. Quite a few gasps were heard round the ballroom. "After all, it's a well known fact that true gentlemen are kind to animals."

"I don't know what you are talking about. You are mad, Charlotte."

"*Lady* Charlotte. And I know you've been inconsolable since I refused your marriage proposal on the grounds of that humiliating report from your physician . . ."

Dudley paled.

Charlotte bit back a triumphant crow. It had been a calculated guess that such a vile creature harbored some disease. As unkind as it was, she hoped it was something slow, painful and incurable. It was also, for the record, a complete fabrication about the marriage proposal.

Color started to reemerge in Dudley's face, from ashen to a faint orange, ripening into a crimson and then swiftly turning into something resembling mashed grapes. His eyes bulged and Charlotte detected a twitch at the corner of his mouth.

The man was enraged.

And the gun remained pointed at her, and her pet.

James, darling beloved utterly mad James, stepped into the fray. Not only that, he stepped between the despicable Dudley and herself.

It looked like she was going to be saved, or rescued, or tragically heartbroken.

She thought about swooning and decided against it.

This was too romantic to miss.

If there had been a doubt in James's mind about marrying Charlotte, the sight of a pistol pointed at her lovely, mad self put the matter entirely to rest. His heart lodged in his throat and his life—their life together—flashed before his eyes, ending before it even began.

He gave her a moment in the spotlight to take her turn extracting revenge on Dudley because she would never forgive James for taking that from her. But he edged closer all the while for the inevitable moment when Charlotte was just a bit too . . . Charlotte.

That was when he stepped in between his future wife (not that she knew it yet) and his former friend.

"Dudley, put the gun down. It is the lady's pet," James said in the sort of voice that left no room for negotiation. Or so he had intended. Dudley had always been a selfish blockhead.

"Pet? Pet? That is clearly a wild, rabid animal and it is scaring the ladies," Dudley replied which was laughable because Dudley was not known to demonstrate the slightest concern for the feelings of others, particularly of women.

"The matter is not negotiable, Dudley. Lower your damned pistol," James said, this time his voice more tense, more angry. His hands clenched into fists. His jaw held firm.

"How cute. Defending the eccentric debutant and her mangy pet," Dudley retorted.

Charlotte issued a garbled sound of rage.

And then Harriet . . .

Oh, Harriet.

She crept up toward Dudley from behind, bearing a curious weapon in her shaking hands. James noticed splashes of the liquid sloshing down the sides of the silver pitcher, undoubtedly smearing the essential message of *west drawing room* that had been inked there earlier.

Clearly Harriet had a trick up her sleeve. She stepped even closer to Dudley, who took no notice of the shy, retiring wallflower. She stepped just to the side of him—and still he was sneering and brandishing his pistol like a madman and carrying on about defending the guests from wild vermin scurrying about in their midst.

Harriet tossed the entire pitcher of lemonade in Dudley's face.

James took that moment to lunge, knocking Dudley to the ground and delivering precisely six devastating blows to the man's jaw and nose. One for George Coney the First, one for his threats against George Coney the Second, one for Penelope, two for Charlotte and one more just because the man was awful and deserved a lot worse.

James then fought to wrench the pistol from Dudley's grasp. He grabbed the man by his wrist and slammed it onto the parquet floor, where just minutes before he'd been waltzing with a beautiful woman in his arms.

The pistol went off.

A bullet pierced the chandelier, shattering a few crystals and sending a flurry of glass shards to the ground.

Women screamed. Men screamed too.

Penelope terrorized everyone with one of those screaming barks and lunged for the rabbit, which recovered its wits and dashed out to the terrace and into the garden. The fox followed.

"Penelope!" Charlotte cried, rushing after her.

"Charlotte!" James yelled, running after her.

Brandon and a few others took care of disposing of Dudley, who was certainly ruined socially forever. It was the least he deserved.

And Charlotte . . . James dashed after her into the garden. Ahead, she picked up her skirts and hurried after Penelope, who at first stuck to the gravel path but then took to leaping over raised garden beds and low hedges, all in pursuit of that vexing rabbit.

Finally, the rabbit discovered a safe retreat in the hollow of a gnarly old oak tree and the fox barked and scratched and otherwise haunted the poor thing.

Charlotte leaned against the tree, gasping for breath.

"Are you all right?" James ventured as he approached Charlotte.

"All right?" Charlotte echoed. "All right?!"

Charlotte's thoughts were racing, her heart was racing, everything was racing like mad and it took a moment before she could do anything other than repeat what he had said.

"Oh, James, I've never been better," she said breathlessly. "That was marvelous!"

Yet another ball interrupted. Dudley getting his comeuppance. A wild animal chase through a ballroom and at least seven people fainting. And now here she was in the garden, alone with James, on a moonlit night. Did life get any better than this?

"I'm so glad you think so," he said. She thought he seemed relieved and grateful.

Charlotte smiled mysteriously at him.

"I wonder if it is a coincidence that there is a rabbit hopping through the ballroom on the same evening George Coney is reputed to be in attendance," she remarked.

"I daresay you are the only one who would," James replied, *still* not confessing to any sort of scheme. She had to admire him for that.

"You might also find it remarkable," she suggested, speaking of their shared history of mischief.

"I might," he agreed and she saw a grin tugging at his lips. God, his mouth was just . . . it gave a girl *thoughts*, mainly of kissing. And not just on the mouth.

"I wonder if this is part of a scheme," she mused, smiling prettily at him.

"You would," he muttered, laughingly.

"You wouldn't?"

James leaned against the tree, and gave her a devastating smile.

"The question, Charlotte, is why?"

This caught her by surprise. She hadn't ever stopped to wonder the *why* of the scheme. And now that he mentioned it, *why* had he brought a rabbit to the party and Lord only knew what else was in the works.

"Why?" she asked.

"Why would a man go to all the trouble of arranging a rumored reading of a book that doesn't exist, by an author who definitely does not exist—at least not in human form. Why would a man bring such a gift with such a special meaning, known only to us . . ."

"And arrange for a fox chase, fisticuffs and the vanquishment of my mortal enemy . . ." Charlotte added dreamily.

"Well that part wasn't planned, though I really should have thought of it," James concurred. And then he said, urgently, "But, Charlotte, I have to tell you something."

"I knew it," she whispered.

He grinned, in that didn't-want-to-but-couldn't-help-it way. She knew the expression well.

What he said took her breath away and set her heart afluttering like never before.

"I love you, Char. I love how clever and imaginative and courageous you are. How kindhearted, loyal and caring you are. And God, you are beautiful. Ever since our afternoon in the folly, I've thought of little else other than you, and wanting to discover you more.

The tears in her eyes were not summoned at will. They were happy tears, glistening on their own accord because this man knew her. He understood her. He loved her. And he was telling her so in a rather romantic speech in the garden on a moonlit night.

Charlotte never thought this moment would happen for

her, the vexing, eccentric girl. It was all the more sweet that the man she loved should feel the same.

"I am speechless," she whispered. Because she had not anticipated this moment, she had not planned a response.

"A first. I am thrilled," he murmured, clasping her hands and drawing her close.

"I love you, too, you know," she murmured when her lips were just inches from him. A kiss . . . that kiss she so ached for was just within reach.

And then Penelope barked (surely one of the least romantic sounds), still fixated on that rabbit. With just a glance, James and Charlotte paused to collect the animals.

"Let's return these to the house. Follow me," she said. Then they crept through the dark garden, taking the more secluded paths. Charlotte led them to the servants' entrance and together they snuck into the house and up to the third floor, where the family kept their bedchambers. The fox was stowed in a room across the hall—with a door that locked properly—and the rabbit was given refuge in Charlotte's dressing closet.

Suddenly, she was alone in her bedroom with a man.

James Beauchamp. Notorious rake. Who loved her.

Her heart started to pound.

"Now where were we?" James asked in a sultry voice that sent shivers tingling up and down her spine. It was also the sultry sort of voice that left no mystery to why he was considered such a seductive rogue, such a catch.

"You were declaring your undying love and listing all my marvelous attributes," Charlotte replied coyly. Slightly breathlessly. She felt marvelously out of sorts.

James slowly slid his hand around her waist. Her heart thudded heavily.

"Yes, that may take a while . . ." James said softly with a sweet grin.

She leaned into him, resting her palm on his chest just above his heart.

"And I said I loved you," Charlotte whispered.

He lowered his mouth quite nearly to hers.

"And we were about to kiss . . ." he murmured. And then he did kiss her and it was perfect. She had come to crave the taste of him, and the feel of his mouth upon hers, teasing and taunting and intoxicating all at once.

He didn't stop with a kiss, though. That was the thing with trouble. Once you started, you might as well give it your everything.

Charlotte always gave her everything. She was generous like that. Tonight, with James, would not be an exception. She would give everything and *more*.

Her bedroom windows were open and moonlight filtered in, along with the laughing, chattering sounds from the party guests below. She should not be here, now, with him. It was a dozen kinds of improper, yet it felt right. She felt like she belonged in this man's arms.

James clasped her cheeks in his hands and kissed her hard.

She clasped the fabric of his shirt in her hands and kissed him back.

"I think . . ." James murmured, and she marveled that he could *think* at a time like this. ". . . That your dress should come off."

"If you insist," Charlotte replied cheekily, even though she was in complete agreement. She thought of some other things that should come off—like his jacket, shirt, cravat, breeches . . .

"Turn around," he said gruffly and she did as told, for once.

James swept her hair away from the back of her neck and pressed kisses against the insanely sensitive skin at the nape of her neck. Charlotte's breath hitched, and she closed her eyes to everything except the stunning sensations . . .

His fingers undoing all the buttons, brushing against her bare skin.

His hands, unlacing her corset. She could breathe deeper now, but still she felt light-headed and breathless.

His mouth, pressing kisses on her shoulders, and then down along her spine . . . licking, kissing, claiming the bare skin no one had ever touched. Lower, lower, lower he went until he pressed his lips against the very base of her back and she whirled around.

James knelt before her, grinning wickedly. His hair was tussled, his shirt wrinkled, and he had that scar. But most of all it was that wicked gleam in his eyes that gave him such a roguish air.

"Feeling faint?" he asked with a lift of his brow.

"No. Perhaps. Yes. Why?"

"Because I think you had better lie down," he said and she managed a naughty smile even as her heart raced.

"Do you?" she murmured.

"Oh, I do."

She stepped backward, tempting him to pursue her. He did, divesting himself of his clothes along the way. His evening jacket hit the floor, his cravat was flung over a chair, his shirt simply vanished. Her dress hit the floor.

Charlotte drank in the breathtaking sight of his bare chest, all the magnificent planes and ridges of his muscled torso, putting her fleetingly in mind of the naked statues at the British Museum. *This was better.*

And but a moment later she was lying down and he lowered his weight onto her, trapping her to the mattress. His eyes were dark as he looked into her eyes.

"I hope you weren't thinking of escaping," he murmured, delicately licking her earlobe and making her gasp. There were no thoughts of escaping. In fact, no thoughts at all other than *Yes. Please. More.*

"Perhaps," she whispered, arching beneath him, just to tease him. James groaned and she felt the hard length of him pressing against her. The feel of him, *there*. The feel of him, everywhere . . .

Charlotte had absolutely zero thoughts of escaping.

James rolled to his side, taking her with him. She tentatively pressed her hand against his chest and he murmured "yes" as he explored her, cupping her breast and drawing a gasp from her mouth. She never wanted the sensation to end, and then it did, and then it got better . . .

He kissed her thoroughly, she kissed him back, anticipating . . . everything else . . . His fingers lightly caressed along her belly, and lower, there, stroking softly in a circular pattern that simply drove her mad.

And then when she couldn't take it any longer, he broke the kiss, gave her a wicked grin and put his mouth, *there*, where his hands had been and Charlotte, for once, was shocked.

She lost herself to the hot, wanton sensation of his mouth generously bringing her to dizzying heights of pleasure— slowly, surely, determinedly—until she could stand it no more and she shattered, crying out his name.

Vaguely, she became aware of the party sounds from below, stealing in through the open window. She became aware again of James as he once again lowered his weight onto hers. She wrapped her arms around him, wanting to feel his bare skin hot against hers.

She was insatiable. She wanted more, more, more . . .

"Charlotte . . ." he whispered her name.

She felt him hot and hard, against her, there.

"Yes," she whispered because in this dreamy, most satisfied, mostly ravished state she still craved more . . . She wanted him, and she wanted him to be satisfied by her. She wanted this, all of it, all of him, now and forever.

Slowly, he entered her. Slowly, she let herself go, and just felt . . . complete. He thrust harder, she gasped. He entwined his fingers in her hair and kissed her again. He moved inside of her, and the pressure built again. She wrapped her legs around his back, he pushed in deeper, she cried out. And then she lost herself completely in the rhythm and the overwhelming sensations until she was crying his name again, and he was capturing it with his kiss. And then James groaned her name and found his release and they both collapsed, sated.

That was definitely trouble. And Charlotte definitely wanted more.

It had never been like that.

James lay with Charlotte in his arms, willing his pounding heart to slow, his lungs to stop gasping for air and fighting sleep all the while. He'd made love, and it had never been like this—for the love of it, with real love, and a sense of play and trouble. And by God, Charlotte, probably didn't know how devastatingly beautiful she was in the moonlight and how her touch undid him.

It was a good thing they were going to be married.

His heart stopped.

First comes love, then comes a *proposal* and then comes marriage.

At that very moment, the clock struck midnight.

He sat up with a start, a tangle of bed sheets around his waist.

"Get dressed, we have to go," he said, trying to get out of bed.

"Mmm. I want to stay here, with you," she said, wrapping her arms around him and kissing him. Oh God, he wanted that too, but first . . .

He reluctantly disentangled himself and began searching for their clothes.

"Is it the reading? It can't happen. Not since George Coney is trapped in the closet," she said, laughing. "What are you rushing around for?"

"Trust me, Charlotte. You don't want to miss this," James said as he frantically pulled on his breeches. *All* the work he'd gone to in creating this dramatic proposal and they both quite nearly missed it!

"Well now I am intrigued," Charlotte remarked, still lying abed. He paused for a moment to preserve the memory: her dark hair against the pillows, her pink cheeks, her lips red from his kiss.

"It'd be even better if you were dressed," he said. Where the devil was his cravat? As he searched, Charlotte quit the bed and began to dress.

Quickly he buttoned up her gown and might have missed a few, but there was no time to fix it. Her hair was a wreck and he grabbed her hand and pulled her away from a comb and the mirror. It was abundantly clear what she had been up to.

He as well, for that matter. His shirt was wrinkled, his cravat hopelessly limp and merely draped around his neck, and his jacket definitely appeared to have spent time on the floor. Under a herd of elephants.

"Oh, I look like I've been ravished," she said, glancing at her reflection in the mirror. It was the truth. He wanted to make love to her all over again. But they could not.

"The look suits you," he said, quickly kissing her cheek. "Now let's go."

Hamilton House

The Corridor

Hand in hand, James and Charlotte dashed through the halls, dodging groups of guests who eagerly ventured to the east drawing room, or the library or God only knew where for the reading of *The Hare Raising Adventures of George Coney* (which did not exist) by George Coney (who was presently locked in Charlotte's closet). It was mayhem at Hamilton House.

He had another destination in mind.

"Where are you taking me?" Charlotte asked breathlessly.

He skidded to a stop on the marble floor.

"I'm not quite sure," he said. "That is, I know *where* I want to take you but not exactly *how* to get there. This house is insanely large."

Charlotte nodded with understanding.

"Once we discovered a family of gypsies living in the north wing. They had been there for a fortnight before discovery," she said gravely.

"And how did they end up there?" James asked with a lift of his brow.

"I couldn't very well let them starve on the streets in a blizzard, now could I?" she replied with a sweet smile and shrug of her shoulders.

"Promise me . . ." he said, and then he stopped.

"Promise you what?"

It was too soon for promises like that, for one thing.

"Harriet! You're supposed to be . . ." James said and he stopped himself again before he revealed their secret destination and when he saw that Harriet was in quite a state.

"What is wrong? Why are you crying?" Charlotte asked, clasping her friend's hand.

"I couldn't find Charlotte anywhere!" Harriet sobbed. "And I looked, and then I couldn't remember which room because of my and . . . oh! Did I miss it?"

The trio glanced curiously at each other. Harriet was particularly focused on James's hand. Holding Charlotte's.

"Miss what?" Charlotte asked, clearly suspicious.

"Um, the reading?" Harriet ventured.

"The reading? Ah yes, the reading by George Coney the rabbit who is currently locked in my dressing closet," Charlotte said. "That very one?"

"The reading has not started yet," James said confidently. Then he winked at Harriet so everything was very clear.

"Oh, thank goodness," Harriet said, heaving a sigh. "I couldn't remember if it was in the east drawing room or the west drawing room. Then I thought it might be in the library after all."

"What, the reading?" Charlotte asked, but everyone ignored her. It was easiest, given the magnitude of the secret they only had to keep for approximately four more minutes.

"Let's go," he said confidently. Then he led Charlotte off down the hall. Harriet followed.

"So it's the east drawing room then," Charlotte said, and he turned around and the two ladies followed wordlessly. The house was just too large.

This observation was reaffirmed when, finally, four minutes later they stood before the heavy double oak doors leading to the west drawing room.

Harriet peeked through the keyhole.

"Yes, this is it," she confirmed.

"It's what?" Charlotte asked, starting to sound very exasperated now.

"See for yourself," James said, hoping he sounded normal when in fact he was nervous. This wasn't just a scheme, it was a proposal.

The West Drawing Room

Charlotte knew there was a scheme in the works. There was no denying it now. Anticipation gripped her and would not let go. Already, it was the most marvelous, magical evening of her life—revenge! Ballroom high jinks! A confession of love and making love! Could it get any better? What the devil else did James have up his sleeve?

Eagerly, she pushed open the doors to the west drawing room and for the second time that evening—and for the second time in her twenty years of age—she was speechless.

She looked around the room and only one word came to mind:

Love.

First she saw the faces of her nearest and dearest: Sophie and Brandon, the other Writing Girls and their rogues, Harriet. And James. James with his hair tussled from bed. His jacket wrinkled from its stint on her bedroom floor. His cravat long gone . . . He looked like such a gorgeous rogue. And he loved her!

Next she saw all the bouquets of freshly plucked flowers—pink peonies, red roses, white lilacs, sweet William and dozens more. There were candles, too, bathing the room in a warm glow. This was *exactly* how she would set up a romantic encounter. And he had read it in her mind and done it for her.

"I knew there was a scheme," she whispered. Because she was still herself and needed it to be known that she hadn't been completely outsmarted.

And then there was James, smiling.

"Charlotte," James said, dropping to one knee and suddenly everything—*everything*—made sense. Not just the schemes of the evening, or the hand of destiny interfering with her previous schemes in just the right ways, but she was meant for this man, and he for her. They had found each other, lost each other and found each other again.

"I love you Charlotte. I had a speech planned for this moment, but I said it earlier this evening. Plans do have a way of going awry, don't they?"

"Sometimes they go just right," Charlotte said with a little nervous laugh. She had thought she would be an eccentric old crone, alone. Yet now she had found a man to love, to cherish, to belong with. James. She loved him. She loved being with him.

"I love you, Charlotte. You are beautiful, vexing, amazing, and I want to spend the rest of my life with you. Will you marry me, Charlotte?"

"Yes," Charlotte said. "But I will not promise to obey."

"I wouldn't dream of asking," James said, laughing.

"Then yes, yes, yes," she cried and flung herself into his outstretched arms. He pulled her close for a kiss, which was promptly interrupted by applause and cheers as a tactful and cheerful reminder that they had an audience.

"You do so love a scene," he said.

"Oh, I do. Everyone must know that I had the most romantic proposal," Charlotte said.

"Oh, and one more thing," James said, pulling a diamond and gold ring from his pocket and sliding it on her finger.

"Oooh," Charlotte cooed as she held her hand up to the light and watched the diamond sparkle in the candle-glow.

"Actually, one more thing," James said, and she barely

wrenched her hand away from the sparkling diamond to see that James had that wicked, mischievous gleam in his eye. That made her heartbeat quicken. *What else could there possibly be?*

Her imagination was at a loss.

Then James handed her a book. Not just any book. The Book.

The Hare Raising Adventures of George Coney by George Coney.

"It's the first volume from the first printing. In fact, it's the only volume at all. Written by the author George Coney who is, ahem, not with us at present due to unforeseen fox hunts," James said. Everyone laughed at that, none more than Charlotte.

"You have to read it, Char," he said when she was still transfixed over the cover: the title embossed in gold on a forest green leather cover. Books were expensive. Books covered in leather and embossed with gold were outrageously costly. A single custom book was an exorbitant sum.

Carefully, she turned to the title page, which made clear that it was the first book, of the first—and only—edition of one.

She turned to the next page, where the story—their story—began.

"Once upon a time, in 1811, there was a mischievous queen named Charlotte," she began in a soft voice.

"And a wicked prince named James," he read.

"They had an inordinate number of dramatic adventures . . ." she read.

Charlotte and James sat upon the settee, reading through this one of a kind book, written by a prince for his queen, featuring all of their best adventures beginning with the rescue of George Coney the First, their spy missions of the summer of 1812, the frog incident (one mustn't ask about that), Captain Beauchamp's Inland Pirate Tree-House-Lair and Lady Charlotte's Ladies Guide to Disposing of Governesses, Penelope's merry chase through Hyde Park and all concluding with that one, perfect, magical line . . .

". . . and they lived happily ever after."

Want to learn more about the
Writing Girls and their escapades?

Continue reading for excerpts from all four books
in Maya Rodale's fabulous series.

An Excerpt from

A GROOM OF ONE'S OWN

On Her Way Down the Aisle . . .

Chesham, Buckinghamshire, England
June 1822

If she is to marry, a woman must have a dowry and a groom of her own. At an exquisitely inconvenient moment, Miss Sophie Harlow discovered one essential prerequisite was deserting her.

To be jilted at the altar is the sort of thing that happens to someone's cousin's friend's sister; in other words, it is something that only occurs in rumors and gossip. It never actually happened to anyone, and it couldn't possibly be happening to *her*.

Yet here she stood in her new satin wedding gown, hearing the words, "I am deeply sorry, Sophie, but I cannot marry you after all," from the man who ought to be saying, "I do."

She could not quite believe it.

Sophie was vaguely aware of the curious expressions of her guests. The Chesham church—small, quaint, centuries-old, and well-to-do like the town itself—was packed with friends from the village, extended family members, and visitors from surrounding counties, as many wished to witness the nuptials uniting two of the most prominent families of the local landed gentry.

Of course they were wondering why the groom had stopped the bride halfway down the aisle. Of course they strained to hear what he said in a voice too low to be audible to anyone else.

She saw her dearest friend, Lady Julianna Somerset, in attendance and as curious and concerned as the rest. Even the church cat, Pumpkin, looked intrigued as she peeked out from underneath a pew.

"I am so sorry to cause you such misery," Matthew repeated quietly, looking pained. His brown eyes were rimmed with red, his skin ashen. His dark hair was brushed forward and tousled in the usual style for a rakish young man. His lips were full and tender, even as he said the bitterest things.

Sophie tried to breathe deeply but her corset would not allow it. She was very glad for the veil obscuring her face.

Misery, indeed.

Her brain was in a fog, and she was pained by every little crack in her heart as it was breaking. Behind the veil, her eyes were hot with tears. Her palms were damp underneath her gloves. The cloying aroma of the lilacs in her bridal bouquet was unbearable, so she let them fall onto the stone floor.

It was her wedding day, and he was leaving her. For the occasion, she wore a new cream-colored satin gown with the fashionable high waist and short puffed sleeves, and the delicate lace veil worn by generations of Harlow brides. Flowers decorated the church pews and beeswax candles added to the gentle late-morning light streaming through the stained-glass windows.

All her worldly possessions were packed up in anticipation of the move from her parents' home to her husband's. And now the dress and flowers were for nothing, and her belongings were packed to go nowhere.

"But why? And when did you . . . and what happened and . . . *why?*" Sophie sputtered.

No one could be expected to form coherent thought in a moment like this.

"Marriage is . . . it's such a commitment . . ."

Obviously.

". . . and I haven't experienced enough. I'm not ready yet. There's so much out there I haven't seen, or done, or . . . I haven't really lived, Sophie," Matthew stuttered while he toyed with the polished brass buttons on his brocade waistcoat. He'd lost enormous sums at cards because of this nervous habit. It had vexed her before, but she loathed it now.

"Hadn't you considered this *before* you proposed? Or in the entire year that we've been betrothed? Or before I started walking down the aisle? Honestly, Matthew, you only realized this *now?*" Sophie tried, and failed, to keep her voice low. Why she bothered, she knew not. This was not destined to remain a secret.

She was not going to spend the rest of her days as Mrs. Matthew Fletcher after all, but as "Poor Sophie Harlow" or "That girl that got jilted."

Sophie turned to go, keenly aware that all eyes were on her. Matthew followed.

"How could you do this to me?" she asked once they were in the vestibule of the church, which provided a modicum of privacy from the dozens of prying eyes. Their curiosity was understandable; she would be nearly falling out of her seat straining to hear, too. Presently, however, she was pacing.

"I know my timing is terrible," he said. "But we have been together for so long already."

Six months of courtship, and a one-year engagement, to be precise. From the time she made her debut, she had wanted Matthew Fletcher; no one else would do. She had turned down two offers of marriage waiting for him to notice her, and two more as he courted her.

Now she was twenty-one and damaged goods. Sophie the Spinster did, alas, have a ring to it.

"And we were about to spend the rest of our lives together," he continued.

"Yes, I am aware of that," she snapped, never ceasing in her steps back and forth like ringing church bells.

"But there is still more for me to experience before I settle down with one woman for the rest of my days," he said, attempting to explain. It was something in the way he said "one woman" that caught her attention. At that, she paused.

"Who is she, Matthew?" Sophie asked coolly.

He looked in the direction of the heavens.

"Matthew."

"With Lavinia, I feel as I have never felt before! We only became acquainted a fortnight ago, and yet . . ." He could not meet her gaze. His fingers were fiddling with the buttons again.

"Lavinia?" It was a horrible, stupid name.

"We became acquainted at the Swan," he said, referring to the inn five miles over in Amersham. "She lost her husband and is now traveling. She has extended an invitation to me to travel with her."

"Matthew, I'm afraid I don't quite understand. You're leaving *me*—your sweetheart, your fiancée, your bride—for a woman you met at an inn less than a month ago?"

Matthew did not say anything, but his silence was answer enough.

"Oh God," she whispered as the truth began to take hold. All the tiny cracks in her heart added up and now the whole thing crumbled into dust. Sophie clutched her hands over her chest and sank to her knees. Her wedding gown billowed around her on the stone floor.

She had loved him, promised herself to him and entrusted him with her heart and her future. And he was leaving her and the life they had planned.

He murmured her name and attempted to console her by snaking his arm around her waist.

"No."

She shrugged off his hands, for she could not bear to be touched by him now, when he likely had held another woman with those arms and kissed another woman with those lips.

And yet, for more than a year, his arms and his kisses had been the surest comfort she had known. He had stolen that from her, too, at the moment when she needed it most.

Traitorous, heartbreaking bounder.

"Sophie," he whispered, "I'm so sorry."

"Oh! How could you!" She stood suddenly, and he did as well.

"Sophie, I—"

She smacked him on the shoulder. "How could you do this to me?"

"I'm so sorry," he repeated. She didn't want to hear it. He could apologize a thousand times with his sad brown eyes and she doubted she could ever forgive him for this.

She balled her hands into fists and pummeled his chest. "How could you do this to *us?*"

Matthew didn't try to stop her, but he did take a step back. Sophie took one step forward, fists flying all the while. In that manner, they started down the aisle. She might just make it to the altar after all—by beating her unwilling groom every step of the way.

Almost.

Matthew tripped over the bridal bouquet she had dropped in the aisle and he began to tumble backward. With flailing arms he reached out for something to steady himself, and grasped onto Sophie's veil, the very one worn by generations of Harlow brides. He took it with him as he fell, mussing up her elaborately arranged hair and tearing the old, delicate family heirloom.

A hush fell over the church. Not a sound from the entryway to the candles and flowers at the altar, from the hard wooden pews to the high, vaulted ceiling—save for heavy footsteps thudding toward her.

"Sophie, stand back," her brother, Edward, declared as he marched toward her.

"What are you doing?" she asked as he helped Matthew to his feet.

The thud of her brother's fist against Matthew's face and the hideous crack of his jawbone was her answer.

And with that, all hell broke loose.

Edward pulled Matthew up and planted another facer on him, sending him falling once more. He knocked into the vicar, who stumbled and stepped on Pumpkin's tail. The poor cat yowled and leapt onto the overly decorated bonnet of Mrs. Beaverbrooke, who shrieked once at the initial shock and again when she saw the damage done. The cat jumped from lap to lap, eliciting shouts and cries in her wake.

Mrs. Harlow fainted. Sophie's father was heard arguing with Mr. Fletcher. Matthew's brothers joined the fray, and the guests quit the pews to crowd around. Someone stepped on Sophie's gown and she cringed at the sound of satin tearing. A baby was wailing. The vicar repeated "Let's calm down now" to absolutely no effect.

Sophie was left alone in a torn gown with a damaged veil, forgotten by all.

"You are still standing at least," Julianna said as she arrived at Sophie's side.

They were the very best of friends—born a month apart, raised only a half-mile apart. They learned to walk together and talk together. Sometimes Sophie thought that Julianna knew her better than she knew herself. She was the one person she needed right now, the one who would understand this betrayal, the one who would know what to do.

"I'm never going to live this down, am I?" Sophie remarked dryly as she surveyed the mayhem unfolding.

"I'm afraid they will be talking about it for decades," Julianna answered in her typically forthright manner.

There would be talk, naturally. The story of Matthew throwing her over at the last possible minute and the subsequent mayhem would spread far and wide. She would not be able to go into any town within four counties without stares, whispers or snide remarks. No man would willingly bind himself to a woman with such a reputation, and a woman was *nothing* without a good, honest, and scandal-free name.

"What do I do now?" Sophie asked. Honestly, she didn't know. From the day she was born, her parents had raised her to one purpose: marry, and marry well.

"There is only one thing, really," Julianna said confidently, linking their arms together and guiding Sophie through the crowd toward the door. "You must come with me to London."

CHAPTER ONE

During a Mad Dash From a Wedding . . .

St. George's Church
Hanover Square, London
One year later, 1823

It was the last place she wanted to be, but no marriage in high life would be complete without Miss Sophie Harlow. This time last year, she had been fleeing from her own disastrous wedding. Now she reported on everyone else's.

Her life had taken a shocking change of direction, and she was occasionally still stunned by it. A combination of heartache, madness, humiliation and a desire to begin anew had driven her to this grand city where she knew no one, save for her dearest friend.

Within a week of her arrival in London, it was clear that she would need an income, for she hated living on Julianna's limited funds provided by her late husband's estate, and the prospect of starving was equally distasteful. Her options for employment were to be a seamstress, servant, governess or mistress and none appealed to her.

Out of desperation, Sophie had done the unthinkable and applied for a man's job—the position of secretary to Mr. Derek Knightly, the publisher of the town's wildly popular newspaper, *The London Weekly*. It had been an outrageous act, and unlikely prospect, but Sophie decided to take the risk.

Even now, a year later, she couldn't quite believe she had done so. Like all girls of a certain social standing, Sophie had been raised to marry advantageously. To work . . . well, it was unthinkable! But so was starving.

Surprisingly, Sophie had left the interview with an offer from Mr. Knightly to write about the one thing she feared most: weddings. Though she had been raised to be a wife, Sophie became a writer.

No man would do it, Mr. Knightly had said. She wouldn't do it either, if it weren't for her other less desirable options of *seamstress or servant, governess or mistress.*

Thus, she became the Miss Harlow of the regular column "Miss Harlow's Marriage in High Life." Inspired by Sophie, Julianna had also turned to writing and had secured a gossip column: "Fashionable Intelligence" by A Lady of Distinction. They, along with Eliza Fielding and Annabelle Swift, were the Writing Girls—and within weeks of their debut in the pages of *The London Weekly*, had become famous.

Mr. Knightly had a hunch that women writers would be scandalous, and that scandals would translate to sales. He was right.

It was all very glamorous except for the small requirement of attending wedding after wedding after wedding . . .

Sophie sat at the end of a pew, toward the wall, away from

the center aisle where the bride would pass. It was an escapable position.

Julianna was by her side, surreptitiously taking in everything that might be gossiped about: who wore what, who conversed with whom, who was in attendance, and who was not.

Everyone looked happy. Pleasant. It was a lovely morning in June and two people in love were going to unite in holy matrimony and presumably live happily ever after.

Sophie felt sick. She never got used to it. Weddings. The nerves. This was her third ceremony of the day—everyone always got married before noon on Saturdays, with a few exceptions—and this was, thankfully, the last one. Still, she was treated with the usual swell and sequence of horrid feelings.

Her stomach tightened into a knot. Her palms became clammy. She was remembering another wedding in June and the slow breaking of her heart as everyone stared on with curiosity and pity. *Breathe*, she commanded herself.

Inhale. She fanned herself with the voucher required to gain admittance—a violation of etiquette, but absolutely essential. *Exhale*.

Seamstress or servant, governess or mistress . . .

She chanted this sequence of her alternative professions, which generally soothed her like a lullaby. As soon as the bride joined the groom at the altar, her feelings would subside. Until that moment . . .

"Still?" Julianna queried. Sophie's breaths were labored and her lips were moving ever so slightly: *seamstress or servant, governess or mistress . . .*

Sophie only nodded, suspecting that she looked ready to be carted off to Bedlam.

"My God, I would like to grievously maim that vile bounder," Julianna said. And though she had made a certain peace with the man who had jilted her, at the moment Sophie's feelings were the same.

"You have spoken my mind," Sophie said.

"Of course, if he hadn't abandoned you like that, then you wouldn't have joined me in London, and we wouldn't be making newspaper history, so we might say that old Matthew Fletcher has done us a favor."

Sophie looked murderously at her friend. As lovely as life in London was—with amazing parties, plays, shops, and company—she'd give it all up in a second for the love of a good, reliable, honest husband.

"Or we might not," Julianna continued.

"What is taking so long?" Sophie asked in a whisper. This is when she became exceptionally nervous—when people were late, and when it seemed like the ceremony might not go smoothly. When someone might, say, *be jilted in front of everyone.*

Honestly, this was not to be endured!

"Probably a torn hem or something insignificant—oh my lord, he is *not*!" Julianna exclaimed.

"What is it?" Sophie asked.

"The groom is leaving the altar," Julianna explained excitedly. The din of hundreds of guests chattering grew louder. This ought to have been welcome news, for it would make splendid additions to their columns. But Sophie's heart—or what was left of it—ached too much.

Sophie forced herself to breathe. "Grievously maimed" would not be sufficient for Fletcher; Sophie was thinking murder now. One year later and she still could not sit through a wedding without suffering the most severe agonies!

"Where is the bride?" she asked her tall friend, who could see much more than she.

"No sign of her," Julianna answered.

"I cannot stay for this," Sophie whispered. She stood up and stepped easily into the far aisle, congratulating herself on having had the foresight to take this seat.

"But your column!" Julianna reminded her, and those seated nearby turned to look at the author of "Miss Harlow's Marriage in High Life," whispering excitedly about seeing her at the wedding.

"Take notes for me. Please," Sophie pleaded, and gave her paper and pencil to her friend.

Sophie kept her gaze low as she rushed out of the church. On a good day she could barely stand it, and today it was all too much. Her only thought was to get away before she began to cry, for this time last year she had fled from a different church, under different circumstances. Perhaps one day she might leave a church with a groom of her own on her arm.

The bright sunlight was blinding as she stepped outside, but Sophie forged ahead through a crowd waiting in expectation to catch a glimpse of the bride and the aristocrats in attendance. She rushed away from Hanover Square toward Piccadilly with eyes to the ground and oblivious to everything until a woman's scream brought her to a halt.

CHAPTER TWO

One Month Before the Wedding . . .

White's Gentleman's Club
St. James's Street, London

"An English gentleman is someone who knows exactly when to stop being one," Lord Roxbury declared. His companions—the usual assortment of peers, second sons, and rakes of all sorts—heartily expressed their agreement.

Henry William Cameron Hamilton kept his disagreement to himself. As tenth Duke of Hamilton and Brandon, he did not have the luxury of even a momentary lapse in gentlemanly behavior. Thus, he never drank overmuch, nor made foolish wagers, nor made an ass of himself over a woman. Vice and excess were strangers to him. Reckless behavior was just not done.

"An English gentleman is someone who knows—" Lord Biddulph did not manage to complete the sentence for falling over drunk. His head thudded onto the tabletop, and his limp arm sent a crystal glass falling and shattering on the floor. His comrades erupted in uproarious laughter.

Brandon, as he was known, noted that it was before noon.

He folded the newspaper he had been reading and set it aside. His friend, Lord Roxbury, caught his eye from across the room and raised his glass of brandy to him, an invitation for Brandon to join them. Regretfully, he declined. Account books were awaiting his review, and doing sums after the consumption of alcohol was not one of his talents.

Though they were his peers in age and in social standing, Brandon felt worlds apart and years older. He had once been as rakish and carefree as the next until he had inherited at eighteen. There had been a time when he certainly would have joined them.

Brandon didn't particularly miss drinking himself into a stupor before dusk, and carousing with opera singers and actresses. He did miss having the liberty to do so without much care for the consequences.

He had forgotten what it felt like to make a decision without considering the effect it would have on his mother, three sisters, the household staff, and the hundreds of tenants who relied upon his judgment and good sense. He wondered what it would be like to feel no obligation to the ancient legacy he had a duty to perpetuate.

To forget he was a duke.

To just be . . . himself.

Brandon did not give voice to such thoughts because no one ever wanted to hear the trials and tribulations of a man of his position. Instead, he took his leave of the others and stepped out of the dark, smoky haven of his club and into the sunshine.

Returning to Hamilton House to balance account books was the last thing any sane person would want to do on a fine summer day like this one. But it had to be done, although a long walk home would be a fine compromise.

As he passed Burlington Arcade, his attention was caught by a woman's scream. She was pointing to another woman in a pale blue dress dashing toward certain disaster. At the sound of the shriek, the girl paused, idiotically frozen with fear, as a carriage pulled by a team of six white horses charged directly toward her.

Brandon bolted forward, knocking over a youth selling newssheets, and sending the gray papers flying high. He lunged forward, grasped her waist with both hands, and yanked her out of the way. She crashed against his chest, knocking the air out of him.

The horses thundered past and the carriage followed.

He held her in his arms. He had saved her.

Brandon held her close for a second longer than was necessary or proper, in part because she made no move to escape and admittedly because she was warm and luscious in his arms. After a moment, he eased her to her feet and let her go. By then a crowd had gathered. He suspected a scene, and he frowned.

But then Brandon caught a glimpse of her plump pink lips and dark curls underneath her bonnet, and the corners of his mouth reluctantly turned up.

"Thank you," she said faintly. She took a deep breath— and his gaze was drawn to the rise and fall of her breasts. He sucked in his own breath. And then she tilted her head back to look up at him with velvety dark brown eyes.

"You saved my life," she said. Her voice wavered. Her pink lips formed a slight smile. She was in shock, but so was he.

For a moment, neither moved.

The longer he looked at her, the more the clatter of the horses' hooves on the cobblestones, the shouts of the merchants, the shoves of the pedestrians all faded, and he was only conscious of an irrational wish to kiss her.

Brandon's heart was pounding and his breath scarce . . . from his recent exertions, of course. It certainly wasn't because of her full, luscious mouth.

He told himself that his inability to breathe had nothing to do with her large brown eyes shadowed by dark lashes, and the way they widened as she looked at him.

Her cheeks were pink, and he wondered if it was because of the sun, or something else?

Brandon yearned to sink his fingers into the mass of dark, glossy ringlets framing her face, to urge her close enough so that he could kiss her.

Here. Now. On one of the busiest streets in London.

That had nothing to do with why his heart was thudding heavily.

He could not lie—it had everything to do with it. He was unfathomably, suddenly, and overwhelmingly entranced by this daydreaming girl who had nearly been trampled by a team of horses.

"Where are we going, miss? I shall escort you," Brandon said. It was clear she was a danger to herself and others, and thus, it was his duty as a gentleman to offer his protection. That, and he did not want to part with her just yet.

"We are not going anywhere," she answered, with an uneven smile. She still seemed a bit pale underneath that blush, almost feverish, and certainly still affected by her near-death experience. "Though I thank you for the offer. You've helped me so much already, I couldn't possibly ask any more of you."

In his opinion, it was very clear that she desperately needed him.

"Surely you are not rebuffing my chivalrous offer of assistance." No one ever refused him anything. He was one of the most respected and powerful dukes in the land.

But she didn't know that, did she? No, she most likely did not. His lips curved into a smile. Once, just once, he would indulge and talk to the pretty girl as if he hadn't a dozen reasons not to. What harm could come from an hour's walk and conversation with her? It seemed likely that plenty of harm would come to her if he did not.

"I abhor the thought of you putting yourself out any more on my account," she said.

"What if I phrased my offer anew? I'm looking for an excuse to stay outside as long as possible on this fine day."

"I am a bit distracted," she admitted with a mischievous sparkle dawning in her eyes. "And I am feeling quite out of sorts, as you might imagine."

Of course. But was she also as stunned by him as he was by her?

"It would be my pleasure to see you safely to your destination."

"Do you have a nefarious purpose in doing so?" She eyed him suspiciously, and it might have been the first time that anyone questioned his integrity. It was oddly thrilling. "Or are you really an honest gentleman intent upon helping a lady?"

"I have nothing but noble intentions," he recited. "I am a notoriously upstanding gentleman. However, if you prefer,

I will procure a hackney for you. Or I shall leave you to your own devices."

Though he did not wish to, Brandon offered to let her go even though he was incredibly and inexplicably keen to remain in her company.

"I should like to walk," she said. And then she gave him a long, hard look as if she could determine his moral worth from that alone, and finally she nodded, and her lips formed a pretty little smile. "You may escort me if you wish, but only because you need an excuse to stay outside today and because I owe you a favor."

"Fair enough," he said, exhaling a breath he hadn't realized he was holding. He understood that it was an incredibly delicate situation for a woman to accept the company of a man she did not know, and publicly. But he had just saved her life, and that had to count for something. He suspected she was thinking the same.

And then there was *something* about her that begged for more of his attentions, and for this one hour he was *not* going to be a Perfect and Proper Gentleman.

"Lead the way, my lady."

They started down Piccadilly, toward Regent Street, walking side by side and weaving their way through the masses of pedestrians crowding the streets.

"It's Miss Harlow, actually. Thank you again for saving me. I do believe that makes you my hero," she said with a smile.

"My pleasure. Call me Brandon," he said. "I'm curious to know what has you so distracted."

"It has been one of those years, Mr. Brandon." At that, she issued a heartfelt sigh, and once again, like a cad, his gaze settled upon the rise and fall of her breasts. He was sorry for her distress, but happy for the sigh.

"You must explain, Miss Harlow," he urged, more intrigued by her with each passing moment.

"This time last year I nearly died from mortification, and just today I nearly died from my own stupidity."

Brandon laughed at that, and she smiled, too, but there was still something akin to sadness in her eyes.

"Are you often found to be dashing about London, alone, and distracted—or is today a special occasion?" he asked.

"Rest assured, it is not a habit of mine."

"Glad to hear it. Did you not at least bring a maid with you?"

"I usually do, but circumstances did not permit it today," she said, and she looked away. It was clear to him that she wasn't just an idiotic female not attending to her surroundings. Something had upset her, sending her running.

Brandon wanted to know what had happened, so he could solve the problem for her. He wanted to protect her, from anything and everything. And yet he didn't even know her. He was not surprised when she changed the subject before he could offer to help her.

"I hate to pry, but may I ask what you are avoiding at home?" she asked politely.

"Women never hate to pry," he answered truthfully, and she laughed. It was not the prettiest of laughs, but it was undoubtedly genuine and thus, a pleasure to hear.

"True," she conceded. "We only say so as to sound polite while we seek to unearth all your secrets. So tell me, Mr. Brandon, what are you avoiding at home?"

"Balancing an accounts book," he answered frankly. *And drafting bills for Parliament, managing six estates, carrying the weight of the world.*

And a fiancée. One of the very good reasons why he should not be conversing with Miss Harlow. Lady Clarissa Richmond was a lovely person and would make a perfect duchess, but she did not intrigue him or arouse him the way this dark beauty beside him did. Of course, that is exactly why he proposed to Clarissa—she was not distracting or demanding, which was exactly what he wanted in a wife.

Miss Harlow was merely a pleasant afternoon diversion.

"Say no more, I beg of you. Shall we take the long way, Mr. Brandon?" She tilted her head to look up at him. The expression on her face was one of innocence, but the spark in her eyes was pure mischief. He grinned. He liked her. For one afternoon, he would be an imperfect gentleman and do exactly as he wished.

"Let's take the long way, Miss Harlow."

Intrigued? Discover more about A Groom of One's Own *at* http://www.mayarodale.com/.

An Excerpt from

A TALE OF TWO LOVERS

CHAPTER ONE

London, 1823

THE BACKSTAGE of the Drury Lane playhouse was no place
for ladies, but Julianna, Lady Somerset, had suffered enough
of what proper women did and did not do. She adjusted the
short veil slightly obscuring her face, clung to the shadows
and kept her eyes wide open for scandal.

She had seen the notorious Lord Roxbury exit this way.
Without a second thought, she followed him. In her experience, to rely on a man was the height of folly—unless it was
to count on Lord Roxbury to get tangled up in a scandalous situation. He was a godsend to gossip columnists everywhere.

It was widely suspected but never confirmed that Julianna
was the infamous Lady of Distinction, author of the column
"Fashionable Intelligence" for the town's most popular newspaper, *The London Weekly*. Since that was, in fact, the truth,
she was on a perpetual quest for gossip.

Thus, if Lord Roxbury went skulking off backstage at
Drury Lane, she followed.

She sought a tall man who moved with confidence and

radiated charm. His hair was black and slightly tousled, as if he'd just gotten out of bed. Frankly, he probably had. Many a woman had sighed over his eyes—plain brown, in her opinion. And his mouth was another subject of intense adoration by women who either had kissed this infamous, glorious rake or longed to do so.

Julianna Somerset could not be counted among the legions of ladies who fawned over him. Her heart and body belonged to no man—not after she had survived a love match gone wretchedly wrong. Like Roxbury and his ilk, the late Lord Somerset was a charmer, a seducer, a man of many great passions, and ultimately a heartbreaker.

Julianna had tasted true love once; it had a remarkably bitter aftertaste.

But that was all in the past. Julianna no longer had to sit at home wondering where her husband was, whom he was with, and how their love had faded to nothing. Other people's business was her focus now.

Hence the following of Lord Roxbury, backstage at Drury Lane, late at night. A man like that could only be up to no good.

"Ah, there you are!"

Julianna turned to see Alistair Grey, her companion for the evening. He reviewed plays for the same paper and they often attended the theater together. Tonight they had seen *She Would and She Would Not*, starring their friend, the renowned actress, "Mrs." Jocelyn Kemble.

"Have you discovered anyone in compromising positions yet?" Alistair asked in a low voice, linking his arm with hers.

"Everyone is on their best behavior this evening," Julianna

lamented softly. "But I swear that I saw Roxbury dash off this way."

"I don't know how you see anything with that veil in this light," Alistair said.

"I see plenty. Certain things are hard to miss," Julianna replied. She had a gift for eavesdropping and an eye for compromising positions and drunken antics. Dim lighting and a black mesh veil did nothing to diminish her talents.

"This hall is desolate, Julianna. Let's go back to the dressing rooms where everyone is drinking and in various states of undress. Surely you'll find more to write about there than in this dark and dusty corridor."

"Yes, but I saw a couple go off this way, and the man looked just like Roxbury. You know how he is," she persisted. That, and she didn't particularly want to be in a crowded dressing room with a half dozen women in their underclothes and two dozen men ogling them.

"I know, but it's probably just some prop mistress and a third son of an impoverished nobleman," Alistair said dismissively.

"In other words, nothing remarkable," Julianna said, heaving a sigh.

The low rumble of a man's laugh broke the silence. In the dark, Julianna gave Alistair a pointed look that said, "I told you so." Together they crept closer, always taking care to remain in the shadows.

There was just enough light from a sconce high on the wall to discern a couple embracing. It was not the wisest position—in a corridor, near a light—she thought, when there were certainly darker and more anonymous locations here for a little romp. But one could be overwhelmed by passion anywhere. Her own deceased husband had been overwhelmed with passion while driving his carriage, and that was the last thing he ever did. In fact, he had been overwhelmed with passion quite frequently, though never with her.

Pushing aside bitter memories of her past, Julianna stepped closer, intent upon discerning their identities. The couple might only be theater underlings but if perchance one of them was a Person of Consequence, she would certainly need to report it.

What she saw shocked even her.

Two pairs of shiny black Hessians, two pairs of breeches-clad legs, two linen shirts coming undone, two dark coats hanging open.

"Oh, my . . ." Julianna murmured under her breath.

As her eyes adjusted to the light overhead, she identified their position: One—tall and dark-haired—clasped the other around the waist, from behind, pulling his partner flush against him. As for the other one . . . his hands were splayed upon the wall, supporting them both, arching his back, turning his head back to accept the kiss of his mysterious male paramour.

Julianna grasped Alistair's arm, giving it a squeeze.

This was beyond scandalous.

This was the sort of item that would cement her reputation as the very best.

It would be a serious blow to her archrival, the infamous gossip columnist at The London Times otherwise known as the Man About Town. He would never be able to top this!

Julianna cursed her veil and stepped forward to gain a closer look. In the process, she tripped over a broom that someone had left carelessly propped against the wall. She swore under her breath.

It clattered onto the floor. The couple jerked apart and instinctively turned in her direction. One man's face was obscured, ducking behind the other for cover. Thanks to the light above she could see the other man's face clearly.

Oh Lord above! Lord Roxbury! With a man!

An earl's only son embracing another man was *news*. In her head she began to compose her column:

Has London's legendary rake, Lord R— so thoroughly exhausted the women of the ton that he must now move on to the stronger sex? Indeed, dear readers, you would not believe what this author has seen . . .

CHAPTER TWO

Carlyle House

A few days later

LIKE MOST GENTLEMEN of his acquaintance, Simon Sinclair, Viscount Roxbury, was equally averse to both matrimony and poverty. His chief aim was to live and die a wealthy bachelor. He had succeeded admirably thus far.

However, his father, the lofty, prestigious, and esteemed Earl of Carlyle had vastly different expectations for his sons' futures. The eldest had expired, and now Roxbury's life, particularly his matrimonial state, was the earl's focus. It was a constant point of disagreement.

Whereas the son was a gallant and charming rake, the elder was a solid, reputable man who dutifully took up his seat in parliament, tended to his estates and gave his wife plenty of pin money but otherwise ignored her. As long as she had new gowns, jewels and a circle of friends, Lady Carlyle cared not for much else.

Roxbury lived in mortal terror that his life should be the same.

He craved passion and lived for the thrills of falling in love . . . over and over again.

Roxbury crumpled the note summoning him to his father's study for another lecture on the duties of a proper heir: not blowing through the fortune, getting married, and producing brats. He deliberately dropped the ball of paper onto the Aubusson carpet in one small sign of defiance.

They would always be father and son, but Roxbury was not to be ordered around like a child any longer.

"You are aware, of course, that I am able to receive correspondence at my residence," Roxbury began. "Sending a summons to my club is really unnecessary."

He had received the missive yesterday afternoon, as he was enjoying a game of cards with some fellows at White's. Roxbury only now found the time to venture over—after a soiree last night and a very leisurely lie-in with the delightful (and flexible) Lady Sheldon this morning.

On his way from her bedchamber to his father's study, Roxbury had paid call upon some of his acquaintances and paramours. None had been at home to him, which was deeply troubling. Not to be boastful, but he was a popular, well-liked fellow. No one ever refused his calls. He could not dwell on it now, though.

"It is necessary to send word to your club," his father said, with the sort of patient tone one reserves for toddlers or the mentally infirm. "Lord knows I could not possibly anticipate which woman's bedchamber you would be in. You certainly are never at your own horrifically decorated residence."

That was true on all counts. A series of angry mistresses had taken their vengeance by decorating the rooms of his townhouse in a uniquely wretched way, with each room worse than the last. There was an excessive amount of gold, and a revolting quantity of red velvet furniture. Roxbury vaguely understood that it was a desperate plea for his attention as the relationship wound down and his eye wandered to other women. However, he generally avoided thinking about it at all costs.

Thus, he preferred to spend his days at his club and his nights with other women. He'd been in three different women's bedchambers this past week alone. Or was it only two? It seemed ungentlemanly to keep count.

Funny, then, that he should have been refused by two or three women this morning. He frowned.

Roxbury loved women. Their lilting laughs, pouting lips, and mysterious eyes. The smooth curves and contours of a female body never failed to entrance him, as did their soft skin and silky hair. Most women were completely and utterly mad—but always to his endless amusement. Women were beautiful, charming, perplexing, delightful creatures, each in their own unique way. How could he limit his attractions, attentions, and affections to just one?

He couldn't possibly. He did not even try.

"I do not mind paying for your residence, and your allowance," his father droned on. He sat comfortably in a large chair on the other side of his desk. It was warm enough to go without a fire, but the windows were closed, too, lending a stale, suffocating air to the room.

"I thank you for that," Roxbury said politely, even though it was his portion from the family coffers, not some gift or charity. It went with the title—one he never asked for and would rather not have, given what it cost him to get it. The name of Roxbury was just a courtesy until he assumed the name and title of Carlyle—and all the responsibilities that came with it.

"After all, a gentleman must maintain a certain style and standard of living," the earl said as he reached for a cigar from the engraved wooden box on his desk, next to a letter opener fashioned from pure gold and studded with emeralds.

"I heartily agree," Roxbury said, wary of where his father's argument was going. He was fond of his fine things, too, but who wouldn't be?

The earl offered a cigar to his son, who accepted. Something strange was going on, he could just tell. First, those refused calls this morning. Lady Westleigh *never* refused him. And now this rambling from his father about living in style. Deuced unusual.

"Part of the duty of a father—a duty I take very seriously— is to provide for one's children. Fortunately, due to my intelligent management of the Carlyle estates, it's something I am able to do."

"I agree," Roxbury said. "Careful management of estates is essential. I am proud to report that Roxbury Park has been making a small profit of late." It was his own parcel of land that he'd been given at the age of eighteen as a future residence and independent source of income. That was when he'd been the second son, and didn't stand to inherit the vast lands and wealth of all the Earls of Carlyle.

Now, as was custom, he went by one of his father's lesser, spare titles—Viscount Roxbury. It had been Edward's name once, Roxbury thought, but then he shoved aside those memories. Now wasn't the time.

"Congratulations," his father said, and Roxbury did acknowledge a surge of pride at the accomplishment and recognition. It was dogged by a nagging sense of dread. This could not be the purpose of the meeting—there must be something else.

The clock on the mantel clicked loudly.

"You are going to need that money, I fear," his father said. Each word was heavier than the last.

The earl paused to light his cigar from the candelabra on his desk. The flame illuminated the slanting cheeks that puffed and pulled on the cigar until the end was aglow and the old man exhaled.

They had the same high cheekbones. The same black hair, though the elder's was graying. Edward, too, had shared these traits. And like his younger brother, Edward had also inherited a wild temperament and passionate nature from some long forgotten ancestor. How their staid and proper parents had raised such hellions was still a mystery to Simon.

They were down to one hellion, one heir, now.

The three of them had shared the same love of money, too. Money was freedom, comfort, and pleasure. It was a necessity and a luxury all at once. The scent of banknotes or the clink of coins did not excite him, but there was a way a man moved, lived, existed when he had an income—to say nothing of a fortune. He did not want to lose that.

Roxbury lifted one of the candles to light his own cigar.

Women. Money. Marriage. Something nefarious was underfoot, he could just tell.

"I have been fulfilling my duties as a father—providing for you, raising and educating you, etcetera, etcetera. However, you have not been fulfilling your duty as an heir."

Roxbury inhaled and exhaled the smoke in perfect rings, in defiance of the earnest and ominous direction of the conversation they'd had a thousand times before.

"I have given the matter much thought, and discussed it with your mother. We both agree that this is the best course of action."

Obviously, his mother generally agreed with whatever her husband suggested.

His father enjoyed his cigar for a moment, leaving Roxbury sitting and smoking in annoyed suspense.

"You have one month to take a wife of proper birth," the old man said. Roxbury choked on a rush of smoke. His father merely smiled and carried on. "In that time, if you have failed to marry a suitable woman, I shall cease to pay your bills."

"Poverty or matrimony?" Roxbury gasped.

"Precisely," the earl said, with a proud, triumphant smile.

"That can't be legal."

"I don't care. And you can't afford the solicitors to deal with the matter, so the point is moot." The smile broadened.

"This is a devious, manipulative, and—" Roxbury would have gone on to say it was repugnant, a violation of the rights of man, and generally an unsporting thing to do, but he was cut off.

"Frankly, I think it smacks of genius." His father inhaled and exhaled his cigar smoke in a steady stream of gray that promptly faded into the rest of the stale air.

Some animals in the wild ate their young. Apparently, his father would allow his only son to die of starvation or be henpecked to death. Poverty or matrimony indeed!

"It's sneaky, underhanded, and meddling like the worst society matron."

"We have a tradition in this family," the earl continued, his voice now booming once he hit upon one of his favorite subjects. "Roxbury men whore it up with the best of them until the age of thirty when they settle down, marry, and produce heirs. You are two and thirty and show no signs of reforming your behavior."

He could easily marry if he wanted to. Roxbury loved women and they loved him back. Honestly, he could have his pick of any of the adorable, ditzy debutantes because he had money, a title and was not hideous.

But he did not want to marry. He loved women, *plural*. Promising to love a woman, singular—for ever and ever— was something he could not do. At heart, for all his rakish ways, he was a romantic. But he was also a levelheaded realist.

A wife would get in the way of his numerous affairs. A wife would get in the way of his life.

Instead of gallivanting backstage at the theater for all hours, he would have to escort the missus home at the conclusion of the performance. A wife, like his mistresses, would redecorate his townhouse in strange colors like salmon, periwinkle, and harvest gold. A wife would mean brats. And that would definitely be the end of life as he knew it.

Roxbury was quite fond of life as he knew it.

"To hell with tradition." Roxbury stamped out the cigar. Tradition hadn't given a damn about Edward. He was supposed to be the heir who would marry and make brats, and leave the way clear for Roxbury to be a reckless rake until the day he expired, which would ideally happen in the arms of a buxom, comely mistress. But Edward wasn't around anymore. He existed only in a portrait above the mantel in the drawing room and in a few poignant memories.

"I will not have my life's work passed along to one of your idiot cousins because you couldn't be bothered to consort with a proper woman for long enough to put a ring on her finger and a baby in her belly. I will not be failed by both of my sons."

"To hell with your ultimatum," Roxbury said in a ferocious voice before he quit the library and Carlyle House.

CHAPTER THREE

White's Gentlemen's Club

St. James's Street, London

AFTER THAT INCREDIBLY disturbing interview with his father—to say nothing of all those calls that had been inexplicably refused this morning—Roxbury proceeded to White's. A drink was certainly in order, either to toast his rebellion and impending poverty or to enjoy a last hurrah before submitting to the bonds and chains of holy matrimony. He was too blindingly mad to know what to do. Neither option appealed to him.

Marriage—never. Poverty—no, thank you.

He arrived at the same time as Lord Brookes, who arched his brow questioningly and sauntered past, declining to say hello. They frequently boxed together at Gentleman Jack's and had always been on good terms. How strange.

Roxbury sat down at a table with his old friend the Duke of Hamilton and Brandon and some other gents. They were all sipping brandies and reading the newspapers.

All the others left. Promptly.

There was a rush of chairs scraping the hardwood floors as they were pushed back in haste, the sound of glasses thudding on the tabletop and the crinkling of newspapers as all the other gentlemen nearby gathered their things and removed themselves to seats on the far side of the room.

What the devil?

The Duke of Hamilton and Brandon, usually known simply as Brandon and a longtime friend, looked at Roxbury and shook his head.

Ever the attentive servant, Inchbald, who was approximately three hundred years old, brought over a double brandy and intoned, "My Lord, you will need this."

"For the love of God, what is going on?"

What had he done now? Or not done? Did this have anything to do with the ultimatum? The calls this morning?

Brandon merely handed his friend the newspaper he'd been reading. It was *The London Weekly*, a popular news rag that Roxbury wouldn't line his trunk with. In his opinion, the gossip columnist owed her entire career to him, for his antics so often appeared in her column.

He wasn't the only one, of course—she'd taken down Lord Wentworth with a mention of his visits to opium dens, then related the intimate details of Lord Haile's grand marriage proposal to all of London, and broken the news of Susannah Carrington and George Granby's midnight elopement—but Roxbury appeared regularly enough that he could refer to it as a reminder of what he had done the previous week, should he forget.

"At least you have a decent excuse for reading this rubbish," Roxbury muttered. Brandon had married one of *The Weekly's* notorious Writing Girls—then known as Miss Harlow—of the column "Miss Harlow's Marriage in High Life."

Roxbury flipped straight to "Fashionable Intelligence" by A Lady of Distinction on page six.

Roxbury took a sip of his drink, thoughtful. He'd wager that if this Lady of Distinction were forced to print her real name, she wouldn't write half the things she did. Frankly, he was surprised her identity was still a secret. Speculation was rampant, of course, with most of the ton focusing on Lady something or other. That was the sort of drivel he didn't follow.

He possessed a sinking feeling that would soon change.

Roxbury began to read.

Has London's legendary rake, Lord R—, so thoroughly exhausted the women of the ton that he must now move on to the stronger sex?

Roxbury downed his drink in one long gulp, feeling the burn of the brandy and keeping his eyes focused on the page, not daring to look up. Inchbald stood over Roxbury's shoulder with the bottle and promptly refilled his glass.

Indeed, dear readers, you would not believe what this author has seen! Lord R— might have been embracing the lovely J— K—, fresh from the stage in her breeches role in She Would and She Would Not. *Yet for a man whose sensual appetites are notoriously insatiable, one knows not what to think.*

Inchbald poured a much-needed second brandy.

Indeed, it was clear what everyone did think. In fact, it explained all those uneasy glances from the other gents in the club and all those women who were not at home to him this morning.

He shuddered, actually shuddered, to think of the conversations currently raging in drawing rooms all over town. Roxbury took another long swallow, and damn if that didn't burn like nothing else.

Having just consumed two or three brandies within the space of five or six minutes, Roxbury could not see straight or focus on the ramifications of this salacious, malicious lie. That ultimatum . . . marriage or poverty . . . with a man? Or a woman?

One thing was certain: these things were not compatible, and they were not favorable.

How was he supposed to marry when no one was at home to him? How was he supposed to maintain his livelihood if his funds were cut off?

Even with all that alcohol muddling his mind and burning his gut, Roxbury knew beyond a shadow of a doubt that this was bad. This was the sort of scandal one never quite recovered from.

The stench of it would stay with him. Years from now—decades, even—whispers of this would follow in his wake, from club to ballroom and everywhere in between. He would not care so much, were it not for that ultimatum and a lifetime of poverty staring him in the face.

Roxbury set down the paper and Inchbald left the bottle beside it.

"I know it was a woman," Brandon said.

"But you do not doubt that it was me," Roxbury replied.

"I know you," his friend said. They'd been friends since Eton, where Roxbury's elder brother, Edward, had introduced them both to drinking, women, and wagering. At Eton, Roxbury had seduced every eligible female within a ten-mile radius. At university, he was notorious. There was no stopping him when he hit the ton.

Brandon had a point. Simon was well known for his romantic exploits, so it was believable that he would be caught in a compromising position. In fact, Roxbury was a legendary rake who was famously known to carry on affairs and intrigues with half of the women of the ton and they thought he was dallying with a *man*?

It was laughable. So Roxbury laughed.

He laughed long, hard, and doubled over in his seat, attracting even more uncomfortable and irritable looks. Brandon lifted his brow curiously and had a sip of his brandy.

"What, exactly, is so humorous about this situation?" Brandon asked.

"No one can possibly believe that story—not when dozens, hundreds, *thousands* of women could come forward and vouch for me," Roxbury pointed out. Perhaps not thousands but many, many women had firsthand knowledge of his abiding love and devotion to women and the female form.

"I hate to say it, Roxbury, but most of those women are married, and I daresay not one would risk her reputation to vouch for you."

Brandon was a stickler for facts, truths, honesty, and all those things. The burning feeling of rage, remorse, and panic in Simon's gut intensified.

"They weren't *all* married," he pointed out.

"Your reputation in the ton is not going to be saved by the word of women of negotiable affection," Brandon correctly and lamentably stated. Roxbury scowled because his friend was right—the word of an actress, or an opera singer or a demimonde darling was not going to carry much weight with the ton.

"There were some widows," he added. He did enjoy those women who were determined to enjoy what one of them had termed her "hard-earned freedom."

"They need their reputation, Roxbury. No one will confess to an affair with a man of questionable proclivities."

"Bloody hell," Roxbury swore, but the curse was insufficient. If there was no way to defuse this rumor . . . If no one would come forward to his defense . . .

It would be impossible to take a wife, particularly if this morning's rejected social calls were any indication. And if that failed, he was looking at a life of living on credit and dodging debtor's prison. His father, it should be noted, was in remarkably good health so his inheritance was far off indeed, not that he wished the man dead.

"I wouldn't worry. It should all be forgotten eventually," Brandon said casually, sipping his drink.

"I don't have the time," Roxbury said tightly. There was that ultimatum, and the clock was ticking. Granted, he'd just declared to hell with it. But that was when he had a choice and now that had been taken from him.

A life of leisure had been secure an hour ago. Now, he hadn't a prayer of finding a wife, and he could kiss his fortune good-bye, too.

Roxbury finished the brandy in his glass and then took a swig straight from the bottle. Life as he knew it was over. It was a sudden death, and he was reeling in shock, denial, regret, and bone-deep terror at what the future would bring.

And anger, too, because he was powerless to do anything. Marriage was impossible, and a refusal to comply meant little when he lacked the option of agreement. Of course, agreeing to his father's demands was something he didn't ever want to do, but the point of remaining a bachelor was to enjoy legions of beautiful women who probably would not have him now. And then he would be poor, too. Poor and alone.

He wondered if the earl had tried this stunt before, with Edward, and if that had been what sent him off to the navy and off to his death. If anyone thought Roxbury was a hellion . . . then they'd never met his elder brother.

Roxbury took another sip of his drink, silently cursing this impossible situation.

"By God, if it weren't for this damned column, all the debutantes and their mothers would be scheming to have me!"

"You have a high opinion of yourself," Brandon said.

"It's the truth and you know it, and it's not about me but my title, my fortune, and, well, I have been called devilishly handsome. Thank God for that. There's nothing worse than an impoverished lord, except for an ugly one."

"Roxbury, you are insufferable."

"Bloody hell, I'm going to be *poor*. When the old man delivered that ultimatum I never thought—"

Brandon merely took a modest sip of his drink. "What ultimatum?" he asked.

Roxbury explained. And then he lamented.

"I don't even have a choice, or a chance now! All because of a damned newspaper story! All because of that petty, irksome busybody who calls herself the Lady of Distinction! My God, if ever a title was unjustified! With just a few lines of moveable type she has annihilated my prospects, destroyed my future, and sentenced me to a life of poverty!"

"I'm sure someone will have you," Brandon said. "There is always Lady Hortensia Reeves."

Lady Hortensia Reeves left *much* to be desired. Miss Reeves was an agreeable woman; she was also firmly on the shelf, and a very proud collector of all sorts of items from embroidery to stamps, leaves, insects, and other rubbish. Apparently it was all neatly labeled and catalogued, so she was not some run-of-the-mill hoarder but a devoted hobbyist. Her other great interest was him, and her infatuation with him was quite painfully obvious.

Needless to say, Roxbury wanted to marry almost anyone else more than he did Lady Hortensia Reeves. While he did not want to marry at all, he *definitely* did not want to bind himself to just anyone if he had to take a wife. But that was all a moot point because the question of his marriage was now out of his hands and crushed by *The London Weekly*'s "Lady of Distinction."

Roxbury took another long swallow of brandy straight from the bottle. He scowled at the older, stodgier lords that frowned in disapproval at him.

"Really, it is utterly unconscionable what she has done," Roxbury carried on. "It's thoughtless, inconsiderate, unchristian, and damned and downright wrong! This is my life at stake! My choices! My name. *My honor.*"

Roxbury stood suddenly, sending his chair tumbling backward and careening across the floor.

All eyes were upon him. With his hazy, drunken vision he saw the familiar faces of Lord Derby; Biddulph; that old dandy,

Lord Walpole; the Earl of Selborne's heir and a few others. With all their attention fixed upon him, Roxbury felt that he ought to make a statement. And so, with a nod of his noble head and a sweeping wave of his arm he grandly informed his peers:

"Gentlemen, you are all safe from my advances, though your wives are not."

The Lady of Distinction was not the only gossip in town. There was another gossip columnist on the prowl in London. His column had been printed in The London Times for forty years now. Alternately feared, reviled, celebrated, and adored, he was the archrival to the Lady of Distinction and an eternal man of mystery. In all of those forty years, for all the thousands of attempts to guess or discover his identity, no one had succeeded. He was known as The Man About Town, but that was all anyone knew of him.

With her story on Roxbury and his secret male lover, the upstart at The Weekly had won this week. It was all anyone spoke about in the clubs, or drawing rooms, or ballrooms or gaming hells. One by one, they'd raise their brows and lower their voices: *Have you heard the latest about Lord Roxbury?*

The Man About Town was immensely vexed that he'd stayed in the dressing rooms the other night instead of lurking around backstage. But what could he say? There were dozens of ladies in various states of undress.

He pulled on his cigar; his course was clear. He'd need to find Roxbury's lover, and he'd need to figure out who that damned Lady of Distinction was.

But in the meantime, on the other side of the room, The

Man About Town bit back a laugh at Roxbury's drunken declaration. Naturally, he'd seen and heard a lot in his time, and it took much to amuse him these days. With Roxbury, the latest "Fashionable Intelligence," and the Lady of Distinction, The Man About Town sensed that a fantastic scandal had only just begun.

Intrigued? Discover more about A Tale of Two Lovers *at* http://www.mayarodale.com/.

An Excerpt from

THE TATTOOED DUKE

CHAPTER ONE

The Duke Returns

The Docks
London, 1825

THEY SAID HE had been a pirate. It seemed utterly believable. The other rumors about Sebastian Digby, the Duke of Wycliff, were equally riveting. It was said that he had charmed and seduced his way across countries and continents; that there existed no law or woman he couldn't bend to suit his whims; that he had lived among the natives in Tahiti and swam utterly nude in the clear turquoise waters; that he had escaped the dankest of prisons and thoroughly enjoyed himself in a sultan's harem.

A gentleman he clearly was not.

And now this charming, adventurous, scandalous duke had returned home, to London.

Miss Eliza Fielding had joined the throngs on the dock to witness the long—awaited return of this duke, as per the orders of her employer, Mr. Derek Knightly. She wrote for the monstrously popular newspaper he owned and edited,

The London Weekly. In fact, she was one of the four infamous Writing Girls who wrote for the paper. For the moment, at any rate.

If she didn't get this story . . .

Eliza tugged her bonnet lower across her brow to protect against the light drizzle falling and dug her hands into the pockets of her coat.

"If you don't get this story," Mr. Knightly had told her plainly as she stood in his Fleet Street office just yesterday, "I can no longer employ you as a writer for *The London Weekly.* I cannot justify it if you are not submitting publishable works."

It was perfectly logical. It was only business. And yet it felt like a lover's betrayal.

Knightly didn't need to say that she hadn't been turning in any decent stories—they both knew it. Weeks had turned into months, and not one article of hers appeared in its pages.

Oh, she used to write the most marvelous stories—a week in the workhouse undercover to expose the wretched conditions, exclusive interviews with Newgate prisoners condemned to death, detailing the goings-on in a brothel to show what the lives of prostitutes were really like. If there was a truth in need of light, Eliza was up to the task. If adventure, danger, and the dark side of London were involved, so much the better.

Lately she hadn't been inspired. The words wouldn't come. Hours she spent with a quill in hand, dripping splotches of ink on a blank sheet of paper.

But this story . . .

Knightly's assignment was plain: to uncover every last secret of the Duke of Wycliff. All of London was panting for the intimate details of his ten years abroad. It wasn't *just* that he was a duke—and the latest in the long line of "Wicked Wycliffs," as the family was known. That alone would have required column inches of ink. But all those rumors . . .

Had he really been a pirate? Was it true about the harem? Had he been made the chief of a small tribe on a remote island in Polynesia? What of mountains scaled, fires started, and lands explored? More important to the ton, was he looking for a wife?

The questions were plentiful. The answers were hers to discover. But how?

"But how?" she asked Knightly. "He's a duke and I am quite far from that. We don't exactly move in the same circles."

Julianna, Countess Roxbury—fellow Writing Girl and gossip columnist—was far better suited to the task.

"Do you not want this story?" Knightly asked impatiently. She saw him glance at the stack of papers on his desk awaiting his attention.

"Oh, I do," Eliza said passionately. It wasn't the money—Knightly's wages were fair, but not extravagant. There was something about being a Writing Girl: the true friendship, the thrill of pushing the boundaries of what a woman could do in this day and age, the love of chasing a great story and the pleasure of writing, excruciating as it occasionally could be.

She made a living by her own wits, dignity intact, and she was beholden to no one. She would not give that up lightly.

"Figure something out," Knightly told her. "Become his mistress. Bribe his staff. Or better yet, disguise yourself as one of the housemaids. I care not, *but get this damned story.*"

Knightly didn't need to say "or else!" or bandy about idle threats to make his point. The truth was there, clear as day: this was her last chance to write something great or there would only be three Writing Girls.

Thus, she was now here, on the docks along with a mob of Londoners vying to see this long-lost pirate duke. All manner of curiosities were hauled off the ship: exotic creatures, exquisite blossoms and plants, dozens of battered crates with words like *Danger* or *Fragile* or *Incendiary* branded on the boards.

Interesting, to be sure, but nothing compared to the man himself.

Everything about him would cause a scandal.

Then she saw him.

His dark hair was unfashionably long, brushing his shoulders and pulled back in a queue save for some windswept strands that whipped around his sharply slanting cheeks.

His skin was still sun-browned. A tantalizing patch exposed at the nape of his neck—which a gentleman would have covered—begged one to wonder how much of his skin had been exposed to the sultry tropical sun. Had he stripped down to his breeches, baring his chest? Or had the lot of his clothing been deemed too restrictive and discarded?

He wore no cravat at his neck; instead, buttons were left undone on his linen shirt, offering a glimpse of the bare skin of his chest. His gray jacket was worn carelessly opened, as if he did not even notice the drizzling rain.

When he moved, one might catch a glimpse of a sword hanging at his side. One would be wise to assume he carried a knife in his boot or a pistol in his coat pocket.

The story. The story. *The story.*

Even on this damp afternoon, Eliza felt like her nerves were smoldering, sparked by equal parts excitement and fear. It was the feeling she always had at the start of a mission, but this time there was something else.

Something that left her breathless. Something that made her feel the heat all over, even in this cool, wet weather. Something that made it awfully difficult to breathe for a second. Something that made it impossible to wrench her gaze away from the man, the duke, *the story.*

Two men, garbed in dark, rough coats next to her in the crowd began a conversation that Eliza freely eavesdropped on as she kept her gaze fixed upon her quarry. She leaned in, the better to listen to their gruff voices.

"I heard that his household is looking to hire, but chits aren't exactly lining up for the job. I know I told my sister under no circumstances was she to take a job there, duke's household or not."

"Aye? Why is that?" This man's posture and tone said he thought it stupid to refuse a job, particularly from a duke.

"Everyone knows the Wicked Wycliffs like to tup their housemaids and then send 'em packing when they're with child," the other said authoritatively. She wondered where he'd heard gossip like that. Probably from *The London Weekly.*

"More than usual?" the man said, thus pointing out that this was hardly unusual behavior.

"Aye, they're legendary for it. They don't call 'em the Wicked Wycliffs for nothing. And this one, particularly— look at him. Would you want yer sister or your missus working under the same roof as him?"

In unison the three fixed their attention on the duke. He boldly paced the ship's deck with determined strides, coat thrown open to the elements and white shirt now wet and plastered across his wide, flat chest and abdomen. Heat infused Eliza's cheeks and . . . elsewhere.

The duke paused to converse with a rough-looking man with one arm in a sling and one eye covered by a black patch. The very definition of disreputable company.

The duke turned to give an order to the crew as they carried off precious cargo. Eliza knew that he was not captain of the ship, but lud, if he didn't act like he was the lord and master of everything around him.

To say the duke was handsome did not do it justice—even from the distance she viewed him at. He was utterly captivating. Danger, indeed.

"No," the man next to her said. "I wouldn't want any of my womenfolk gettin' near the likes of that."

Eliza smiled, because she would dare to get close. She thought again of Knightly's flippant, impatient words: *Or better yet, disguise yourself as one of the housemaids.*

Her heart pounded as she pieced that together with the gossip she had shamelessly overheard: *I heard that his household is looking to hire, but chits aren't exactly lining up for the job.*

Shivers of excitement. The thrill of the chase. Her job on the line.

Get the story. Get the story. Get the story . . .

On the spot, she made a decision. In order to save her position as one of *The London Weekly*'s Writing Girls, she would disguise herself as a maid in the household of the scandalous, wicked Duke of Wycliff.

The very next day, wearing a plain dress and with fake letters of reference from her fellow Writing Girls, the Duchess of Brandon and the Countess Roxbury, Eliza found herself at work in Wycliff House—dusting the library bookshelves, in particular, while His Grace entertained a caller—where she would have unfettered access to the duke, his household, and his secrets . . . and to the shocking story she needed in order to remain a writer at *The London Weekly*.

CHAPTER TWO

In Which There Is Nudity

Wycliff House

WITHIN FOUR-AND-TWENTY HOURS of his return to English soil, Sebastian Digby, the new Duke of Wycliff, had a caller. His idiot cousin Basil had come to visit. Worse, Basil brought a decade's worth of gossip and a deplorable inability to discern the interesting from the mundane.

Sebastian—still not used to the name Wycliff applied to himself—had once been held in an Egyptian prison with a man who insisted on telling the long, excruciatingly dull history of herding cattle in the desert. Basil's company and conversation rivaled that for sleep inducing properties.

Nevertheless, in proper English fashion they took tea before the fireplace on another damp, gray March afternoon.

A maid dusted the bookshelves. She had a very nice backside. Such was the saving grace of the afternoon.

Basil rambled on. He reported all the major scandals—marriages, a divorce, duels and deaths—and briefly mentioned news regarding Lady Althea Shackley. At the mention of her name, Wycliff shifted uncomfortably in his chair.

Basil then mentioned the creditors plaguing the household and loitering in front of the house. News that the duke had returned spread like the plague, and hordes of merchants crawled out of the woodwork to demand payments owed for services rendered by the previous duke, or that had accumulated whilst Wycliff was adventuring on the far side of the world.

Wycliff knew he would have to do something about them. Pay them, presumably.

Or swiftly depart for lands unknown. He was leaning toward the latter. Timbuktu, in particular.

"We had all given you up for dead," Basil began. "Though rumors would float back every now and then."

"We?"

"Myself, my missus, the rest of the ton," Basil explained. "But then we all heard rumors of your adventures and whereabouts. Is it true that you spent a week in a harem ravishing a hundred concubines of the sultan?"

Gossip apparently was not much troubled by distance.

Nearby, the maid with the lovely bottom slowed with her dusting, as if she were eavesdropping. He assumed so; anyone would be. Dull as Basil might be, he was far more interesting than dusting.

Wycliff grinned at the memory of the one exquisite night of unbridled passion kindled by the grave threat of discovery. Some things were worth risking life and limb for.

"It was only one night," he clarified. The maid coughed. Aye, she was listening. And doing the math.

"That's the sort of rumors and gossip that will have the ton matrons in a tizzy," Basil remarked. He bit into a biscuit and brushed the bread crumbs from his puce-colored waistcoat.

"That's what I do, Basil," Sebastian replied. He always had. It's what the Wycliffs had done for generations. There wasn't a more outrageous, debauched, devil-may-care clan in England's history. The men were notorious for dallying with the household maids, for spending fortunes on mistresses, and for generally being a drunken, undisciplined lot. Oddly enough, they tended to marry stern, practical, cold wives. The sort that *might* manage to impose some order and civilizing behavior. None had ever managed to do so.

His own parents were no exception. By some miracle, he had inherited his mother's rigid self-control, and it warred constantly with his Wicked Wycliff blood.

"I suppose it doesn't take much to upset the ton," Basil conceded. He clearly took after the other side of the family. The dull side. "Now what about those rumors that you were a pirate?"

"What about them?" Wycliff asked, lifting his brow suggestively just to provoke his cousin. He ought to invite Harlan to join them. Basil would surely be aghast at the man's eye patch, injured arm, and pirate charade. He wondered if the parrot had survived the journey from Fiji to London to Wycliff House.

"Will you not deny it?" Basil asked, his voice tinged with glee. "And do tell about Tahiti. I heard that's where they found you."

"Warm crystal blue waters sparkling on white sand beaches, incessant sunshine, loose, barely clad women. It gets a bit boring after a while," Wycliff said with a shrug. Monroe Burke, friend and rival, had found him there with the news of the previous duke's passing. Or, the news that he had a reason to return after a decade abroad.

"You were bored in a tropical paradise and returned to England to claim your dukedom," Basil stated. "Hmmph."

"Such is life . . ." Wycliff mused. He was supposed to feel guilty about his travels and adventures, but he had refused. He knew he was supposed to thank his bloody stars he'd been born a duke, but more often than not it felt more like a burden than a blessing. Instead, he went after what he wanted in life, dukedom be damned. Was that such a crime, or was it a well-lived life?

The maid glanced over her shoulder, and even with her face in profile he could see her scowl. That, and her delicate English features and a creamy complexion. A little pink rosebud of a mouth. Her hair was dark and pulled into a tight knot at the base of her neck. Wycliff wanted to see more. He wanted to see her eyes.

"Well, best of luck to you upon reentering society," Basil said, casting a critical eye on Wycliff's appearance. "You'll have to cut your hair, of course. And you will never get into Almack's with . . . with . . . that *earring*."

Little did Basil know, the small gold hoop—a sailor's traditional burial funds—was the least of the decoration he'd picked up on his travels.

"Of all the placed I've traveled to, from Africa to Australia, and Almack's is the one that's inaccessible to me," Wycliff drawled. "Pity, that."

The maid couldn't restrain a bubble of laughter. Definitely listening.

"If you want a wife and an heir, you'll have to venture to Almack's. Brave that, or else everything shall go to me!" Basil said with a touch of glee. "Sure would please my missus."

Wycliff glanced at the maid, who lifted her brow, silently suggesting that he'd do best to take a wife rather than leave an entire dukedom to *Basil*, for Lord's sake.

"Not that there is much to inherit, given the bothersome creditors by your door," Basil added. "Still, my missus would fancy herself a duchess."

Wycliff's expression darkened. Then he reminded himself that he wouldn't care about Basil inheriting because he himself would be dead. Quite frankly, that was the Wycliff tradition: worry not, for the heirs shall sort out the mess with the mortgaged estates, rampant debt, rebellious tenants, etc, etc.

Bastards.

The maid kept dusting—had it not been done in years?—moving on now toward his desk. Being bored and women-starved, Wycliff freely ogled her bottom and the hourglass shape of her hips. Her eyes, though—he wished to see her eyes. A man could tell so much about a woman by her eyes.

"But you must take a wife, if only for the fortune," Basil continued, and Wycliff did not disagree with him. "First, you'll need to cut your hair, visit Saville Row for proper attire—"

Wycliff wore plain buckskin breeches and a shirt that was open at the collar and rolled at the sleeves. His boots had carried him through Africa, pounded the decks of dozens of ships, waded through swamps and seas alike. Frankly, his clothing looked like it had suffered all that and worse.

"I thought it was enough to be a duke," he interrupted rudely.

"Sometimes it is," Basil replied. "But if you are desperate . . ."

"I am not desperate."

In fact, he had no intention of shackling himself. He had other plans for his time in England—namely, to plan and seek funding for the expedition of a lifetime, before he set sail once more. But Basil would not accept this, so he didn't even bother to try to persuade his cousin otherwise. Instead he allowed him to carry on.

"Well you ought to find a wife," Basil said. "I'd be delighted to assist you, introduce you around, etcetera."

If he was planning to take a wife, Wycliff mused, telling his idiot cousin would be the first mistake. That was the path to matchmaking disasters and other high society atrocities.

"Thank you, cousin. So very kind of you."

And with that Basil slurped one last sip of tea, set down the cup, and stood to go. Finally, this visit would be over and he could get on with reacclimating himself to his native country. Beginning with the brothels.

Basil ambled through the study, slowing as he neared the desk. Wycliff swore under his breath.

"Don't look," Wycliff muttered. Basil looked. Of course he looked.

"I say, are those drawings of your travels?" his cousin exclaimed. He then took the liberty of lifting one up for a better view.

"Blimey, cousin! What the devil—" Basil's eyes nearly bugged out of his head.

It was a portrait of a girl named Miri; she had graciously allowed him to draw her, including the tattoos that covered her hands, which were clutching her full, luscious breasts. She was laughing in the picture, and he couldn't recall why; he would never know now, unless he sailed back to ask her.

He ignored a pang of longing, like homesickness.

"Tattooing," Wycliff explained. "It's a Tahitian custom that involves sharp bone tapping ink under the skin. It takes days. It's excruciating—" He stopped when Basil's skin adopted a greenish hue, matching his waistcoat.

The maid was angling for a look at the drawing, too, and he grinned, and allowed her to see. He watched her eyes widen and look up to him, searching for answers.

The look knocked the smile off his face and kicked his breath away. Blue. Her eyes were gray-blue like the ocean, where he longed to be.

"I suppose one would expect such customs from the savages," said the idiot cousin. Wycliff rolled his eyes.

"They're not savages, Basil, they are people who happen to live by a different set of cultural practices," he lectured.

"Of course, given your travels you may have a different perspective, but really, no one on earth surpasses the British," Basil replied, riffling through more sheets.

Of someone else's private property. Idiot. Cousin.

The maid bit her lip. She wanted to speak, and Wycliff was very intrigued.

"Well that one is quite a stunner," Basil said, referring to a watercolor of Orama, a lovely woman with soft lips and a warm embrace, who had allowed him to sketch her nude form as she rose like Aphrodite from the ocean with the turquoise water lapping around her hips. She was breathtaking, and it was some vile mistake that his idiot cousin Basil should be able to look at such raw beauty.

Out of the corner of his eye Wycliff saw the little maid's cheeks turn pink. He'd forgotten how adorably prudish and modest English women could be.

Wycliff took the sheet away from Basil, and the other sketches, "For all your talk of civilized behavior in England, it seems quite uncivilized to sort through a man's personal papers."

"Indeed, indeed. I say, my apologies. One just has such a curiosity for all things exotic. You'll have to join me at my club, cousin, and tell my friends of your travels," Basil offered. Wycliff muttered something like agreement, even though he had no desire to sit around a stuffy old club with stuffy old men.

Finally, after much ado, Basil was gone and he was alone with the maid. She curtsied awkwardly before him, murmured "Your Grace" and asked if there was anything she could provide him with. All with that little pink mouth of hers. Wicked thoughts crossed his mind, but he would not give voice to those, even though it would be such a typical Wicked Wycliff thing to do.

"If you can, I'd like that hour of my life back," he said frankly.

"If I had the ability to turn back time, I'd have no need of your wages," she replied tartly as she gathered up the tea things. It ought to have been a simple affair, but china cups clattered against sauces and silver spoons clinked across the tray and she spilled the milk. She also swore under her breath, which delighted him. She must have met Harlan already, he thought, or had some unsavory past of her own.

Thus far this little maid with the sea-blue eyes and salty language was the only thing of interest in England.

"What is your name?" he asked.

She hesitated before answering. "Eliza."

With her arms laden with the tea tray, she managed a short, awkward curtsey on her way out, treating him to a splendid view of her backside, again.

Once she was gone, he pulled the key from the leather cord he wore around his neck and used it to unlock and open the door leading from the library to a room otherwise cut off from the rest of the house. It was here that he kept those things he wished no one to see. Not yet.

CHAPTER THREE

In Which the Nudity Is His Grace's

Later that day, dusk

ELIZA STOOD OUTSIDE the door to His Grace's bedchamber, summoning the gumption to walk in unannounced while His Grace was in a bath. Naked. It wasn't as if she'd never seen a naked man before. She wasn't some sheltered missish thing.

The protocol for a situation like this eluded her: a naked duke, in the bath, without a drying cloth. She probably shouldn't go in. Or should she? Having never grown up with servants, nor having been one herself, Eliza was learning everything about her new job the hard way.

She had filled that damned bathtub—hauling heavy buckets of boiling water up three floors—with the help of another housemaid, Jenny. The task required moving fast enough to keep the water warm, but not so fast that they'd spill it. It had been excruciating. The duke had better enjoy his damned bath.

In Eliza's haste and inexperience, she had forgotten to leave a drying cloth. She did not yet know if he was the type to roar and holler in anger, and she did not care to find out, because he was an imposing, intimidating hulk of a man and because she was the type to roar and holler back. That spelled trouble. That spelled *fired*, and she could not lose this position or her story for *The London Weekly*.

Get the story. *Get the story.*

Thus, she debated. Leave him without a drying cloth? Or interrupt?

He hadn't arrived with a valet, or hired one yet, which meant there was no one else to attend to him . . .

Such was the life of a writer, undercover and in disguise. The things she did for Mr. Knightly, and for *The Weekly*! If she had to go to such lengths to get a story published—employed as a housemaid in the most scandalous household in town—then by damn, she would. She would *not* lose her position. Not over this.

She ought to go in, she reasoned. She would not pay attention to him, and he would do the same because she was a servant and thus utterly beneath his notice. That much she knew about master and servant relations. Yet she had a feeling it would not be so simple.

Eliza recalled the way His Grace had looked at her in the study this afternoon, and how his gaze felt like an intimate caress. The man left her breathless.

"Bother it all," she muttered, and entered his chambers. Then she stopped short.

She saw the duke in the bath, as expected. But it was no ordinary sight. His hair was wet and slicked back from his face, showing off strong, hard features. His mouth was full and firm and not smiling. Even in this pose of relaxation, he put her in mind of a warrior: always aware, always ready.

The water lapped at his waist, his chest a wide, exposed expanse of taut skin over sculpted muscle. As Eliza stepped toward him and saw more of the man illuminated by the burning embers in the grate and the flickering of candles, she noticed that his chest was covered in inky blue-black lines. Tattoos, like the drawing.

She gasped. His eyes opened.

"Hello, Eliza." The duke's voice was low, smoky, and sent tremors down her spine. The window was slightly ajar and the cool breeze made the candle flames dance wildly, casting slate-colored shadows, making the room seem like some strange, magical, otherworld.

"Your Grace," she murmured, and bobbed into a curtsey.

"Have you come to join me?" he asked in a rough voice, and she could not tell if he was serious or bamming her.

"My wages don't cover that, either, Your Grace," she replied, not yet having mastered her subservience, but she was rewarded for her impertinence when his mouth curved into a grin.

Eliza's gaze inevitably drifted back to his nudity. The tattooing covered the broad expanse of his muscled chest, wrapping up over the shoulders and generously covering his upper arms, even inching onto his forearms. A million questions were poised on the tip of her tongue. Yet her mouth was suddenly too dry to form words.

"Tattoos," he confirmed, reading her mind. "It's a Tahitian custom. When in Rome . . ."

"You mentioned that it was painful," she said, referring to the exchange earlier. "It seems like it must be."

"Like the devil."

"Why would you do it, then?"

"Because to not do so is considered cowardly," he explained in a low voice.

"That's all? Because you do not wish to be seen as weak in front of men on the far side of the world?"

The duke laughed. "You don't understand men, do you?"

"Apparently not," she replied dryly.

"The sketches are one thing to see; this is another entirely. Wouldn't you agree?" Eliza nodded yes. "It's a record of my travels, and one of many artifacts that I have collected and brought back to England. There's a whole world out there, beyond London. People should know that."

"Can I look closer?" she asked in a whisper, because it seemed too illicit to ask a duke for an intimate glimpse of his person. But she had to see the tattoos up close. If she could touch them, she would. This was the sort of thing *The Weekly* would love. But also, her own curiosity impelled her to seek satisfaction.

Eliza knelt by the tub to see the tattoos, but her attention was also drawn to the scar she noticed on his upper lip, and the stubble upon his jaw. He had a clean, soapy scent that was at odds with the air of danger around him.

His head was close to hers, his mouth only inches away.

She wanted to touch his skin, to know if the tattoos left it rough or smooth. To feel the hard muscles of his arms and his chest underneath her palms. For *The Weekly*, of course.

As if the duke could read her mind, he took her hand and rested it on his bicep, just above where the tattoo began.

With a glance at him for permission, she traced her fingers along the lines—some straight, some jagged, some swirling up and around the curve of his shoulder and leading her down to the expanse of his torso. She splayed her palm across his chest and felt his hot skin and pulsing heartbeat.

The duke's hand closed over hers.

The candles were still wavering, throwing shadows. Steam rose up from the water, making the air hot and humid between them. His lips parted—to kiss her or rebuke her for being so forward?

Her own lips opened to tell him that she was not that kind of girl. Yet Eliza was in the habit of ignoring common sense and better judgment when it came to satisfying her curiosity, chasing a story or embracing adventure. Or men. She had secrets and stories to prove it.

Jenny, the other housemaid, chose that moment to enter the room. There was a sigh of relief—hers or the duke's? Eliza snatched her hand away. The duke leaned back and closed his eyes as she stood and moved away from him to speak to the other maid.

"I was just checking if His Grace was finished," Jenny said in a whisper. "We'll have to remove the tub and water tonight." Then her eyes widened as she noted the duke's tattoos as well. "And you'll need to turn down the bed, and all that. And have a care . . . you know his reputation."

Intrigued? Discover more about *The Tattooed Duke* at http://www.mayarodale.com/.

An Excerpt from

SEDUCING MR. KNIGHTLY

Young Rogue Crashes Earl's Funeral

OBITUARY

Today England mourns the loss of Lord Charles Peregrine Fincher, sixth Earl of Harrowby and one of its finest citizens.

The Morning Post

St. George's Church
London, 1808

DEREK KNIGHTLY HAD not been invited to his father's funeral. Nevertheless, he rode hell for leather from his first term at Cambridge to be there. The service had already commenced when he stalked across the threshold dressed in unrelenting black, still dusty from the road. To remove him would cause a scene.

If there was anything his father's family had loathed—other than him—it was a scene.

The late Earl of Harrowby had expired unexpectedly of

an apoplexy, leaving behind his countess, his heir, and one daughter. He was also succeeded by his beloved mistress of over twenty years, and their son.

Delilah Knightly hadn't wanted to attend; her son tried to persuade her.

"We have every right to be there," he said forcefully. He might not be the heir or even have his father's name, but Derek Knightly was the earl's firstborn and beloved son.

"My grief will not be fodder for gossips, Derek, and if we attend it shall cause a massive scene. Besides, the Harrowby family will be upset. We shall mark his passing privately, just the two of us," she said, patting his hand in a weak consolation. Delilah Knightly, exuberant darling of the London stage, had become a forlorn shell of her former self.

In grief, Knightly couldn't find the words to explain his desperate need to hear the hymns sung in low mournful tones by the congregation, or to throw a handful of cool dirt on the coffin as they lowered it into the earth. The rituals would make it real, otherwise he'd always live with the faint expectation that his father might come round again.

He needed to say good-bye.

Most of all, Derek desperately wanted a bond to his father's other life—including the haute ton where the earl had spent his days and some nights, the younger brother Derek never had adventures with and a younger sister he never teased—so it might not seem like the man was gone entirely and forever.

Whenever young Knightly had asked questions about the other family, the earl would offer sparse details: another son who dutifully learned his lessons and not much else, a sister fond of tea parties with her vast collection of dolls. There was the country estate in Kent that Knightly felt he knew if only by all the vivid stories told to him at night before bed. His father described the inner workings of Parliament over the breakfast table. But mostly the earl wanted to step aside from his proper role and public life to enjoy the woman he loved and his favored child—and forget the rest.

Knightly went to the funeral. Alone.

The doors had been closed. He opened them.

The service had begun. Knightly disrupted it. Hundreds of sadly bowed heads turned back to look at this intruder. He straightened his spine and dared them to oppose his presence with a fierce look from his piercing blue eyes.

He had every right to be here. He belonged here.

Derek caught the eye of the new earl, held it, and grew hot with fury. Daniel Peregrine Fincher, now Lord Harrowby, just sixteen years of age, was a mere two years younger than his bastard half brother who had dared to intrude in polite company. He stood, drawing himself up to his full height, a full six inches less than Derek, and declared in a loud, reedy voice:

"Throw the bastard out. He doesn't belong here."

CHAPTER ONE

A Writing Girl in Distress

DEAR ANNABELLE

Dear Annabelle,
* I desperately need your advice . . .*
* Sincerely,*
* Lonely in London*

*   The London Weekly*

Miss Annabelle Swift's Attic Bedroom
London, 1825

SOME THINGS ARE simply true: the earth rotates around the sun, Monday follows Sunday, and Miss Annabelle Swift loves Mr. Derek Knightly with a passion and purity that would be breathtaking were it not for one other simple truth—Mr. Derek Knightly pays no attention to Miss Annabelle Swift.

It was love at first sight exactly three years, six months, three weeks, and two days ago, upon Annabelle's first foray into the offices of *The London Weekly*. She was the new advice columnist—the lucky girl who had won a contest and the position of Writing Girl number four. She was a shy, unassuming miss—still was, truth be told.

He was the dashing and wickedly handsome editor and owner of the paper. Absolutely still was, truth be told.

In those three years, six months, three weeks, and two days, Knightly seemed utterly unaware of Annabelle's undying affection. She sighed every time he entered the room. Gazed longingly. Blushed furiously should he happen to speak to her. She displayed all the signs of love, and by all accounts, these did not register for him.

By all accounts, it seemed an unwritten law of nature that Mr. Derek Knightly didn't spare a thought for Miss Annabelle Swift. At all. Ever.

And yet, she hoped.

Why did she love him?

To be fair, she did ask herself this from time to time.

Knightly was handsome, of course, breathtakingly and heart-stoppingly so. His hair was dark, like midnight, and he was in the habit of rakishly running his fingers through it, which made him seem faintly disreputable. His eyes were a piercing blue, and looked at the world with an intelligent, brutally honest gaze. His high, slanting cheekbones were like cliffs a girl might throw herself off in a fit of despair.

The man himself was single-minded, ruthless, and obsessed when it came to his newspaper business. He could turn on the charm, if he decided it was worth the bother. He was wealthy beyond imagination.

As an avid reader of romantic novels, Annabelle knew a hero when she saw one. The dark good looks. The power. The wealth. The intensity with which he might love a woman—her—if only he *would*.

But the real reason for her deep and abiding love had nothing to do with his wealth, power, appearance, or even the way he leaned against a table or the way he swaggered into a room. Though who knew the way a man leaned or swaggered could be so . . . *inspiring*?

Derek Knightly was a man who gave a young woman of no consequence a chance to be *something*. Something great. Something special. Something *more*. It went without saying that opportunities for women were not numerous, especially for ones with no connections, like Annabelle. If it weren't for Knightly, she'd be a plain old Spinster Auntie or maybe married to Mr. Nathan Smythe who owned the bakery up the road.

Knightly gave her a chance when no one ever did. He believed in her when she didn't even believe in herself. That was why she loved him.

So the years and weeks and days passed by and Annabelle waited for him to really notice her, even as the facts added up to the heartbreaking truth that he had a blind spot where she was concerned.

Or worse: perhaps he did notice and did not return her affection in the slightest.

A lesser girl might have given up long ago and married the first sensible person who asked. In all honesty, Annabelle had considered encouraging young Mr. Nathan Smythe of the bakery up the road. She at least could have enjoyed a lifetime supply of freshly baked pastries and warm bread.

But she had made her choice to wait for true love. And so she couldn't marry Mr. Smythe and his baked goods as long as she stayed up late reading novels of grand passions, great adventures, and true love, above all. She could not settle for less. She could not marry Mr. Nathan Smythe or anyone else, other than Derek Knightly, because she had given her heart to Knightly three years, six months, three weeks, and two days ago.

And now she lay dying. Unloved. A spinster. A *virgin*.

Her cheeks burned. Was it mortification? Remorse? Or the fever?

She was laying ill in her brother's home in Bloomsbury, London. Downstairs, her brother Thomas meekly hid in his library (it was a sad fact that Swifts were not known for backbone) while his wife, Blanche, shrieked at their children: Watson, Mason, and Fleur. None of them had come to inquire after her health, however. Watson had come to request her help with his sums, Mason asked where she had misplaced his Latin primer, and Fleur had woken Annabelle from a nap to borrow a hair ribbon.

Annabelle lay in her bed, dying, another victim of unrequited love. It was tragic, tragic! In her slim fingers she held a letter from Knightly, blotted with her tears.

Very well, she was not at death's door, merely suffering a wretched head cold. She did have a letter from Knightly but it was hardly the stuff of a young woman's dreams. It read:

Miss Swift—

Annabelle stopped there to scowl. *Everyone* addressed their letters to her as "Dear Annabelle," which was the name of her advice column. Thus, she was the recipient of dozens—hundreds—of letters each week that all began with "Dear Annabelle." To be cheeky and amusing, everyone else in the world had adopted this salutation. Tradesmen sent their bills to her addressed as such.

But not Mr. Knightly! Miss Swift indeed. The rest—the scant rest of it—was worse.

> Miss Swift—
>   Your column is late. Please remedy this with all due haste.
>   D.K.

Annabelle possessed the gift of a prodigious imagination. (Or curse. Sometimes it felt like a curse.) But even she could not spin magic from this letter.

She was never late with her column either, because she knew all the people it would inconvenience: Knightly and the other editors, the printers, the deliverymen, the news agents, all the loyal readers of *The London Weekly*.

She loathed bothering people—ever since she'd been a mere thirteen years old and Blanche decreed to Thomas on their wedding day that "they could keep his orphaned sister so long as she wasn't a nuisance." Stricken with terror at the prospect of being left to the workhouse or the streets, Annabelle bent over backward to be helpful. She acted as governess to her brother's children, assisted Cook with the meal preparation, could be counted on for a favor when anyone asked.

But she was ill! For the first time, she simply didn't have the strength to be concerned with the trials and vexations of others. The exhaustion went bone deep. Perhaps deeper. Perhaps it had reached her soul.

There was a stack of letters on her writing desk across the room, all requesting her help.

Belinda from High Holburn wanted to know how one addressed a duke, should she ever be so lucky to meet one. Marcus wished to know how fast it took to travel from London to Gretna Green "for reasons he couldn't specify." Susie requested a complexion remedy, Nigel asked for advice on how to propose to one sister when he had already been courting the other for six months.

"Annabelle!" Blanche shrieked from the bottom of the stairs leading to her attic bedroom.

She shrunk down and pulled the covers over her head.

"Annabelle, Mason broke a glass, Watson pierced himself and requires a remedy, and Fleur needs her hair curled. Do come at once instead of lazing abed all day!"

"Yes, Blanche," she said faintly.

Annabelle sneezed, and then tears stung at her eyes and she was in quite the mood for a good, well-deserved cry. But then there was that letter from Knightly. Miss Swift, indeed! And the problems of Belinda, Marcus, Susie and Nigel. And Mason, Watson and Fleur. All of which required her help.

What about me? Annabelle thought. The selfish question occurred to her, unbidden. Given her bedridden status, she could not escape it either. She could not dust, or sweep or rearrange her hair ribbons, or read a novel or any other such task she engaged in when she wished to avoid thinking about something unpleasant.

Stubbornly, the nagging question wouldn't leave until it had an answer.

She mulled it over. *What about me?*

"What about me?" She tested the thought with a hoarse whisper.

She was a good person. A kind person. A generous, thoughtful, and helpful person. But here she was, ill and alone, forgotten by the world, dying of unrequited love, a virgin . . .

Well, maybe it was time for others to help Dear Annabelle with her problems!

"Hmmph," she said to no one in particular.

The Swifts were not known for the force of their will, or their gumption. So when the feeling struck, she ran with it before the second-guessing could begin. Metaphorically, of course, given that she was bedridden with illness.

Annabelle dashed off the following column, for print in the most popular newspaper in town:

To the readers of The London Weekly,

 For nearly four years now I have faithfully answered your inquiries on matters great and small. I have advised to the best of my abilities and with goodness in my heart.

 Now I find myself in need of your help. For the past few years I have loved a man from afar, and I fear he has taken no notice of me at all. I know not how to attract his attention and affection. Dear readers, please advise!

  Your humble servant,
  Dear Annabelle

Before she could think twice about it, she sealed the letter and
addressed it to:

> *Mr. Derek Knightly*
> *c/o The London Weekly*
> *57 Fleet Street*
> *London, England*

Chapter Two

Lovelorn Female Vows to Catch a Rogue

The Man About Town

No man knows more about London than Mr. Derek Knightly, infamous proprietor of this newspaper's rival publication. And no one in London knows one whit about him.

The London Times

Offices of The London Weekly
57 Fleet Street, London

Derek Knightly swore by three truths. The first: *Scandal equals sales.* Guided by this principle, he used his inheritance to acquire a second-rate news rag, which he transformed into the most popular, influential newspaper in London, avidly read by both high- and lowborn alike.

The second: *Drama was for the page.* Specifically the printed, stamp-taxed pages of *The London Weekly*, which were filled to the brim with salacious gossip from the ton, theater reviews, domestic and foreign intelligence, and the usual assortment of articles and advertisements. He himself did not partake in the aforementioned scandal or drama. There were days where he hardly existed beyond the pages he edited and published.

The third: *Be beholden to no one.* Whether business or pleasure, Knightly owned—he was not owned. Unlike other newspapers, *The London Weekly* was not paid for by Parliament or political parties. Nor did theaters pay for favorable reviews. He wasn't above taking suppression fees for gossip, depending upon the rumors. He'd fought duels in defense of *The Weekly*'s contents. He'd already taken one bullet for his beloved newspaper and would do so again unblinkingly.

When it came to women—well, suffice it to say his heart belonged to the newspaper and he was intent that no woman should capture it.

These three truths had taken him from being the scandalborne son of an earl and his actress-mistress to one of London's most infamous, influential, and wealthiest men.

Half of everything he'd ever wanted.

For an infinitesimal second, Knight paused, hand on the polished brass doorknob. On the other side of the wooden door, his writers waited for their weekly meeting in which they compared and discussed the stories for the forthcoming issue. He thought about scandal, and sales, and other people's drama. Because, given the news he'd just heard—a *London Times* reporter caught where he shouldn't be—London was about to face the scandal of the year . . . one that threatened to decimate the entire newspaper industry, including *The London Weekly.*

Where others often saw disaster, Knightly saw opportunity. But the emerging facts made him pause to note a feeling of impending doom. The victims in this case were too important, the deception beyond the pale. Someone would pay for it.

With a short exhalation and a square of his shoulders, Knightly pushed opened the door and stepped before his team of writers.

"Ladies first," he said, grinning, as always.

The Writing Girls. His second greatest creation. It had been an impulsive decision to hire Sophie and Julianna to start, later rounded out by Eliza and Annabelle. But the guiding rational was: *Scandal equals sales.*

Women writing were scandalous.

Therefore . . .

His hunch had been correct. The gamble paid off in spades.

The London Weekly was a highbrow meets lowbrow newspaper read by everyone, but the Writing Girls set it apart from all the other news rags by making it especially captivating to the women in London, and particularly attractive to the men.

To his left, Miss Annabelle Swift, advice columnist, sighed. Next to her, Eliza—now the Duchess of Wycliff— gave him a sly glance. Sophie, the Duchess of Brandon—a disgraced country girl when he first met her—propped her chin on her palm and smiled at him. Lady Roxbury brazenly took him on with her clear, focused gaze.

"What's on this week, writers?" he asked.

Lady Julianna Roxbury, known in print as A Lady of Distinction and author of the salacious gossip column "Fashionable Intelligence," clearly had news. "There are rumors," she began excitedly, "of Lady Lydia Marsden's prolonged absence from the ton. Lady Marsden is newly returned to town after she missed what ought to have been her second season. I am investigating."

By investigating, she likely meant all manner of gossip and skulking about, but that was what *Weekly* writers did. Like the writers at *The Times*, but without getting caught.

No one else in the room seemed to care for the significance of a debutante's whereabouts. Knightly barely did, he knew only that it would sell well to the ton. If the news covered one of their own, they talked about it more, which meant that more copies were sold just so people could understand conversations at parties.

To his right, good old Grenville grumbled under his breath. His irritation with the Writing Girls was never far from the surface. If it wasn't the deep, dark inner workings of Parliament, then Grenville wasn't interested.

"Annabelle has quite the update," Sophie interjected excitedly. "Much more interesting than my usual news on weddings."

Knightly turned his attention to Annabelle, the quiet one.

"My column this week has received more letters than any other," she said softly. She held his gaze for a quick second before looking down at the thick stack of correspondence on the table and a sack on the floor at her feet.

He wracked his brain but couldn't remember what she had submitted—oh, it had been late so he quickly reviewed it for errors of grammar and spelling before rushing it straight to the printers. Her work never required much by way of editing. Not like the epics Grenville submitted or the libel Lady Roxbury often handed in.

"Remind me of the topic again?" he said. Clearly, it had resonated with the readers, so he ought to be aware of it.

She blinked her big blue eyes a few times. Perplexed.

There was a beat of hard silence in the room. Like he had said something wrong. So he gave the room A Look tinged with impatience to remind them that he was an extremely busy man and couldn't possibly be expected to remember the contents of each article submitted the previous week for a sixteen-page-long newspaper.

But he could feel the gazes of the crew drilling into him—Owens shaking his head, Julianna's eyebrows arched quite high. Even Grenville frowned.

Annabelle fixed her gaze upon him and said, "How to attract a man's attention."

That was just the sort of thing *Weekly* readers would love—and that could lead to a discussion of feelings—so Knightly gave a nod and said, "Good," and inquired about Damien Owens's police reports and other domestic intelligence. The conversation moved on.

"Before we go," Knightly said at the end, "I heard a rumor that a reporter for *The London Times* has been arrested after having been caught impersonating a physician to the aristocracy."

Shocked gasps ricocheted around the room from one writer to another as the implications dawned. The information this rogue reporter must have gathered from the bedrooms of London's most powerful class . . . the fortune in suppression fees he must have raked in . . . If information was power, suddenly this reporter and this newspaper held all the cards.

There was no way the ton would stand for it.

"That could explain so much." Julianna murmured thoughtfully, her brow knit in concentration. "The broken Dawkins betrothal, Miss Bradley's removal to a convent in France . . ."

This only supported Knightly's suspicions that there would soon be hell to pay. Not just by *The London Times* either.

"Why are you all looking at me?" Eliza Fielding, now the Duchess of Wycliff, inquired.

"Because you were just famously disguised as a servant in a duke's household," Alistair Grey, theater reviewer said, with obvious delight. Eliza grinned wickedly.

"I'm married to him now, so that must grant me some immunity. And I am not the only reporter here who has gone undercover for a story. What about Mr. Owens's report on the Bow Street Runners?"

"That was weeks ago," Owens said dismissively.

"You were impersonating an officer," Eliza persisted.

"Well, has anyone asked Grenville how he obtains access to Parliament?" Owens questioned hotly. All heads swiveled in the direction of the grouchy old writer with the hound-dog face.

"I don't pretend anything, if that's what you're suggesting," Grenville stiffly protested. "I sit in the gallery, like the other reporters."

"And after that?" Owens questioned. "Getting 'lost' in the halls like a 'senile old man'? Bribes for access to Parliament members?"

"We all do what needs to be done for a story," cut in Lady Roxbury, who had once disguised herself as a boy and snuck into White's, the most exclusive and *male* enclave in the world. "We're all potentially on the line if authorities start looking into the matter. But they cannot possibly because then every newspaper would be out of business and we'd all be locked up."

"Except for Miss Swift. She would be safe, for she never does anything wicked," Owens added. Everyone laughed. Even Knightly. He'd wager that Dear Annabelle was the last woman in the world to cause trouble.

CHAPTER THREE

What to Wear When Attracting a Rogue

LETTER TO THE EDITOR

I deplore today's fashions for women, which play to men's baser instincts. Unfortunately, Gentlemen do not seem to share my dismay. I fear for the civilized world.

Signed, A Lady

The London Weekly

IF THERE HAD been the slightest doubt in Annabelle's mind about the dire need to enact her campaign for Knightly's attention, this afternoon's events had dispelled it. Even if she'd been quaking with regrets, consumed by doubts, and feverishly in a panic about her mad scheme, her exchange with Knightly would have cleared her head and confirmed her course of action.

Mission: Attract Knightly must now commence, with every weapon at her disposal. It was either that or resolve herself to a lifetime of spinsterhood. The prospect did not enthrall.

The rest of the staff had quit the room; the Writing Girls stayed. Annabelle remained paralyzed in her place.

"He hadn't read my column," she said, shocked. Still.

She needed to say the wretched truth aloud. If she needed any confirmation of what Knightly thought of her—or didn't—this was all the information she needed. Her own editor, *a man paid to look at her work*, didn't even read it. If it weren't for the thick stack of letters from readers, she might have flung herself off the London Bridge. That was how lonely it felt.

Lord above, it was mortifying, too. Everyone else knew why she sighed when Knightly walked in the room. She was sure they all knew about her inner heartache during her brief exchange with him. How could Knightly not see?

He hadn't read her column, and it had been about him!

"Annabelle, it wasn't that terrible. I'm sure he doesn't read all of our work either," Sophie said consolingly. "Certainly not my reports on weddings."

"It's not just that," Annabelle said glumly. "No one thinks I am wicked."

Julianna, who was very daring and wicked, grinned broadly. "So they shall be all the more speechless when it turns out you are! I loved your column on Saturday. Knightly may not have read it, but the rest of the town did. Your next course of action is being fiercely debated in drawing rooms all over town."

"Indeed?" It was strange to think of strangers debating her innermost vexations.

"There seems to be two schools of thought," Sophie replied. "One suggests that you simply confess to him your feelings."

"I am terrified at the thought," Annabelle replied.

"Then you may be interested in the other method..." Sophie paused dramatically. "Seduction."

"I couldn't possibly," Annabelle scoffed. "That would be wicked, and you heard Owens; I never act thusly."

"He's an ass," Julianna retorted.

Usually Annabelle would have admonished her friend's coarse language. Instead, she said, "No, he's right. I am Good. Therefore, I am not interesting. Why should Knightly take notice of me? There is nothing to notice!"

Wasn't that the plain old truth!

The mirror dared to suggest she was pretty, but all Annabelle saw was a riot of curls that were best restrained in a tight, spinsterish bun atop her head. She did have lovely blue eyes, but more often than not kept her gaze averted lest she draw attention to herself. Furthermore, her wardrobe consisted entirely of brownish-gray dresses made of remnant fabric from her brother's cloth-importing business. To say the cut was flattering or fashionable was to be a liar of the first order.

She might dare think people would see beyond her disastrous hair and hideous dresses. Most of the time she couldn't.

"Oh, Annabelle. You are rather pretty—so pretty that he, like any red-blooded male, should notice you. Unless he's not..."

"See, I am blushing at your mere suggestion!" Annabelle squeaked.

"We do have work to do," Julianna murmured.

"What do your letters say?" Sophie asked, picking one up.

Annabelle scowled and grabbed the first one, reading it aloud.

"'Dear Annabelle, in my humble opinion a low bodice never fails to get a man's eye. It plays to their rutting instincts, which we all know they are slaves to . . . Betsy from Bloomsbury.'"

"A trip to the modiste! I love it." Sophie clapped her hands with glee. But Annabelle frowned. Beggars ought not be choosers, yet . . .

"I want him to notice me for *me*; who I am as a person. Not just bits of me."

"You have to start with certain parts. Then he'll attend to the rest," Julianna replied. "Come, let's go get you a new dress."

"You must wear it for my party later this week," Sophie said, then adding the most crucial detail: "Knightly has been invited."

The opportunity dangled before her like the carrot and the horse. Never mind that the analogy made her a horse. The facts were plain:

There was something she might try (thank you, Betsy from Bloomsbury) and an opportunity at which she might do so (thank you, Sophie, hostess extraordinaire).

She had made that promise to her readers, and it would be dreadful to let them down. She did so despise disappointing people.

Annabelle twirled one errant curl around her finger and mulled it over (Swifts were not known for their quick decisions). She supposed there were worse things than a new gown and a fancy ball. For her readers, she would do this.

Not one hour later, Annabelle was standing in the dressing room of Madame Auteuil's shop. A previous customer had returned a lovely pink gown after a change of heart, and Annabelle wore it now as the seamstresses took measurements for a few alterations.

"I don't think it quite fits," she said. It wasn't the size per se, for she knew it would be tailored to her measurements. It was the dress itself.

It was silk. She never wore silk.

It was pink, like a peony or a rosebud or her cheeks when Knightly spoke to her. She never wore pink.

The pink silk was ruched and cinched and draped in a way that seemed to enhance her every curve and transform her from some gangly girl into a luscious woman.

Annabelle wore simply cut dresses made of boring old wool or cotton. Usually in shades of brown or gray or occasionally even taupe.

The Swift family owned a fabric importing business, which dealt exclusively in plain and serviceable cottons and wools guided by the rational that everyone required those, but so few indulged in silks and satins. Blanche generously provided Annabelle with last season's remnants for the construction of her wardrobe.

This silk, though, was lovely. A crimson silk sash cinched around her waist, enhancing what could only be described as an hourglass figure. It was a wicked color, that crimson.

Madame Auteuil stepped back, folded her arms and appraised her subject with a furrow of her brow and a frown on her lips. She had pins in her mouth and Annabelle worried for her.

"She needs a proper corset," the modiste finally declared. "I cannot work without the lady in the right undergarments."

"A proper corset fixes everything," Sophie concurred.

"And lovely underthings . . ." Julianna smiled with a naughty gleam in her eye.

Annabelle began to do math in her head. Living as glorified household help for her brother and his sister meant that her *Weekly* wages went to her subscription at the circulating library and a few other inconsequential trinkets, and then the rest went into her secret account that Sophie's husband had helped her arrange. It had been her one small act of rebellion.

"I'm not sure that underthings are necessary . . ." Annabelle began to protest. Silk underthings sounded expensive and no one would see them, so how could she justify the expense when she could have a few delicious novels instead?

"Do you have the money?" Eliza asked softly. She was a duchess now, but she'd had anything but an aristocratic upbringing or connections. She understood economies.

"Well, yes. But I feel that I should save," Annabelle said frankly.

"For what?" Eliza asked.

"Something," Annabelle said. Something, someday. She was always waiting and preparing for an event that never came—or had she missed it, given that she didn't know what she was waiting for?

"Annabelle, this is that something," Sophie said grandly. "You want Knightly to notice you, do you not?"

"And you have an occasion to wear it," Eliza said, adding a dose of practicality. "Sophie's soiree, tomorrow night."

"But he won't see my unmentionables. Those needn't be—"

"Well he might, if you are lucky," Julianna said frankly.

And lud, didn't that make her cheeks burn! The thought made her entire body feel feverish, in a not altogether unpleasant way.

"Annabelle," Sophie began, "you must think of fashion as an investment in your future happiness! That is not some silk dress, but a declaration that you are new woman, a young, beautiful woman interested in life! And love!"

"But the underthings?" Annabelle questioned.

"I promise you will love them," Sophie vowed. "You'll see . . ."

In the end, Annabelle was persuaded to purchase one pink silk dress, one blue day dress, one corset that enhanced her person in ways that seemed to violate natural laws, and some pale pink silk unmentionables that were promptly stashed in the back of her armoire.

Intrigued? Discover more about Seducing Mr. Knightly *at* http://www.mayarodale.com/.

ABOUT THE AUTHOR

MAYA RODALE began reading romance novels in college at her mother's insistence and it wasn't long before she was writing her own. Maya is now the author of multiple Regency historical romances. She lives in New York City with her darling dog and a rogue of her own. Please visit her at http://www.mayarodale.com.

Visit www.AuthorTracker.com for exclusive information on your favorite HarperCollins authors.

Give in to your impulses . . .
Read on for a sneak peek at two brand-new
e-book original tales of romance
from Avon Books.
Available now wherever e-books are sold.

THE FORBIDDEN LADY
By Kerrelyn Sparks

TURN TO DARKNESS
By Jaime Rush

An Excerpt from

THE FORBIDDEN LADY

by Kerrelyn Sparks

(Originally published under
the title *For Love or Country*)

Before *New York Times* bestselling author Kerrelyn Sparks
created a world of vampires, there was another world of spies
and romance . . .

Keep reading for a look at her very first novel.

CHAPTER ONE

Tuesday, August 29, 1769

"I say, dear gel, how much do *you* cost?"

Virginia's mouth dropped open. "I—I beg your pardon?"

The bewigged, bejeweled, and bedeviling man who faced her spoke again. "You're a fetching sight and quite sweet-smelling for a wench who has traveled for weeks, imprisoned on this godforsaken ship. I say, what *is* your price?"

She opened her mouth, but nothing came out. The rolling motion of the ship caught her off guard, and she stumbled, widening her stance to keep her balance. This man thought she was for sale? Even though they were on board *The North Star*, a brigantine newly arrived in Boston Harbor with a fresh supply of indentured servants, could he actually mistake her for one of the poor wretched criminals huddled near the front of the ship?

Her first reaction of shock was quickly replaced with anger. It swelled in her chest, heated to a quick boil, and soared past her ruffled neckline to her face, scorching her cheeks 'til she fully expected steam, instead of words, to escape her mouth.

"How . . . how *dare* you!" With gloved hands, she twisted the silken cords of her drawstring purse. "Pray, be gone with you, sir."

"Ah, a saucy one." The gentleman plucked a silver snuffbox from his lavender silk coat. He kept his tall frame erect to avoid flipping his wig, which was powdered with a lavender tint to match his coat. "Tsk, tsk, dear gel, such impertinence is sure to lower your price."

Her mouth fell open again.

Seizing the opportunity, he raised his quizzing glass and examined the conveniently opened orifice. "Hmm, but you do have excellent teeth."

She huffed. "And a sharp tongue to match."

"*Mon Dieu*, a very saucy mouth, indeed." He smiled, displaying straight, white teeth.

A perfectly bright smile, Virginia thought. What a pity his mental faculties were so dim in comparison. But she refrained from responding with an insulting remark. No good could come from stooping to his level of ill manners. She stepped back, intending to leave, but hesitated when he spoke again.

"I do so like your nose. Very becoming and—" He opened his silver box, removed a pinch of snuff with his gloved fingers and sniffed.

She waited for him to finish the sentence. He was a buffoon, to be sure, but she couldn't help but wonder—did he actually like her nose? Over the years, she had endured a great deal of teasing because of the way it turned up on the end.

He snapped his snuffbox shut with a click. "Ah, yes, where was I, becoming and . . . disdainfully haughty. Yes, that's it."

Heat pulsed to her face once more. "I daresay it is not surprising for *you* to admire something *disdainfully haughty*, but regardless of your opinion, it is improper for you to address me so rudely. For that matter, it is highly improper for you to speak to me at all, for need I remind you, sir, we have not been introduced."

He dropped his snuffbox back into his pocket. "Definitely disdainful. And haughty." His mouth curled up, revealing two dimples beneath the rouge on his cheeks.

She glared at the offensive fop. Somehow, she would give him the cut he deserved.

A short man in a brown buckram coat and breeches scurried toward them. "Mr. Stanton! The criminals for sale are over there, sir, near the forecastle. You see the ones in chains?"

Raising his quizzing glass, the lavender dandy pivoted on his high heels and perused the line of shackled prisoners. He shrugged his silk-clad shoulders and glanced back at Virginia with a look of feigned horror. "Oh, dear, what a delightful little *faux pas*. I suppose you're not for sale after all?"

"No, of course not."

"I do beg your pardon." He flipped a lacy, monogrammed handkerchief out of his chest pocket and made a poor attempt to conceal the wide grin on his face.

A heavy, flowery scent emanated from his handkerchief, nearly bowling her over. He was probably one of those people who never bathed, just poured on more perfume. She covered her mouth with a gloved hand and gently coughed.

"Well, no harm done." He waved his handkerchief in the

air. "*C'est la vie* and all that. Would you care for some snuff? 'Tis my own special blend from London, don't you know. We call it *Grey Mouton*."

"Gray sheep?"

"Why, yes. Sink me! You *parlez français*? How utterly charming for one of your class."

Narrowing her eyes, she considered strangling him with the drawstrings of her purse.

He removed the silver engraved box from his pocket and flicked it open. "A pinch, in the interest of peace?" His mouth twitched with amusement.

"No, thank you."

He lifted a pinch to his nose and sniffed. "What did I tell you, Johnson?" he asked the short man in brown buckram at his side. "These Colonials are a stubborn lot, far too eager to take offense"—he sneezed delicately into his lacy handkerchief—"and far too unappreciative of the efforts the mother country makes on their behalf." He slid his closed snuffbox back into his pocket.

Virginia planted her hands on her hips. "You speak, perhaps, of Britain's kindness in providing us with a steady stream of slaves?"

"Slaves?"

She gestured toward the raised platform of the forecastle, where Britain's latest human offering stood in front, chained at the ankles and waiting to be sold.

"Oh." He waved his scented handkerchief in dismissal. "You mean the indentured servants. They're not slaves, my dear, only criminals paying their dues to society. 'Tis the mother country's fervent hope they will be reformed by their experience in America."

"I see. Perhaps we should send the mother country a boatload of American wolves to see if they can be reformed by their experience in Britain?"

His chuckle was surprisingly deep. "*Touché.*"

The deep timbre of his voice reverberated through her skin, striking a chord that hummed from her chest down to her belly. She caught her breath and looked at him more closely. When his eyes met hers, his smile faded away. Time seemed to hold still for a moment as he held her gaze, quietly studying her.

The man in brown cleared his throat.

Virginia blinked and looked away. She breathed deeply to calm her racing heart. Once more, she became aware of the murmur of voices and the screech of sea gulls overhead. What had happened? It must have been the thrill of putting the man in his place that had affected her. Strange, though, that he had happily acknowledged her small victory.

Mr. Stanton gave the man in brown a mildly irritated look, then smiled at her once more. "American wolves, you say? Really, my dear, these people's crimes are too petty to compare them to murderous beasts. Why, Johnson, here, was an indentured servant before becoming my secretary. Were you not, Johnson?"

"Aye, Mr. Stanton," the older man answered. "But I came voluntarily. Not all these people are prisoners. The group to the right doesn't wear chains. They're selling themselves out of desperation."

"There, you see." The dandy spread his gloved hands, palms up, in a gesture of conciliation. "No hard feelings. In fact, I quite trust Johnson here with all my affairs in spite of his criminal background. You know the Colonials are quite wrong in thinking we British are a cold, callous lot."

Virginia gave Mr. Johnson a small, sympathetic smile, letting him know she understood his indenture had not been due to a criminal past. Her own father, faced with starvation and British cruelty, had left his beloved Scottish Highlands as an indentured servant. Her sympathy seemed unnecessary, however, for Mr. Johnson appeared unperturbed by his employer's rudeness. No doubt the poor man had grown accustomed to it.

She gave Mr. Stanton her stoniest of looks. "Thank you for enlightening me."

"My pleasure, dear gel. Now I must take my leave." Without further ado, he ambled toward the group of gaunt, shackled humans, his high-heeled shoes clunking on the ship's wooden deck and his short secretary tagging along behind.

Virginia scowled at his back. The British needed to go home, and the sooner, the better.

"I say, old man." She heard his voice filter back as he addressed his servant. "I do wish the pretty wench were for sale. A bit too saucy, perhaps, but I do so like a challenge. *Quel dommage*, a real pity, don't you know."

A vision of herself tackling the dandy and stuffing his lavender-tinted wig down his throat brought a smile to her lips. She could do it. Sometimes she pinned down her brother when he tormented her. Of course, such behavior might be frowned upon in Boston. This was not the hilly region of North Carolina that the Munro family called home.

And the dandy might prove difficult to knock down. Watching him from the back, she realized how large he was. She grimaced at the lavender bows on his high-heeled pumps. Why would a man that tall need to wear heels? Another pair of lavender bows served as garters, tied over the tabs of his silk knee breeches. His silken hose were too sheer to hide padding, so those calves were truly that muscular. *How odd.*

He didn't mince his steps like one would expect from a fopdoodle, but covered the deck with long, powerful strides, the walk of a man confident in his strength and masculinity.

She found herself examining every inch of him, calculating the amount of hard muscle hidden beneath the silken exterior. What color was his hair under that hideous tinted wig? Probably black, like his eyebrows. His eyes had gleamed like polished pewter, pale against his tanned face.

Her breath caught in her throat. A tanned face? A fop would not spend the necessary hours toiling in the sun that resulted in a bronzed complexion.

This Mr. Stanton was a puzzle.

She shook her head, determined to forget the perplexing man. Yet, if he dressed more like the men back home—tight buckskin breeches, boots, no wig, no lace . . .

The sun bore down with increasing heat, and she pulled her hand-painted fan from her purse and flicked it open. She breathed deeply as she fanned herself. Her face tingled with a mist of salty air and the lingering scent of Mr. Stanton's handkerchief.

She watched with growing suspicion as the man in question postured in front of the women prisoners with his quizzing glass, assessing them with a practiced eye. Oh, dear, what were the horrible man's intentions? She slipped her fan back into her purse and hastened to her father's side.

Jamie Munro was speaking quietly to a fettered youth who appeared a good five years younger than her one and twenty years. "All I ask, young man, is honesty and a good day's work. In exchange, ye'll have food, clean clothes, and a clean pallet."

The spindly boy's eyes lit up, and he licked his dry, chapped lips. "Food?"

Virginia's father nodded. "Aye. Mind you, ye willna be working for me, lad, but for my widowed sister, here, in Boston. Do ye have any experience as a servant?"

The boy lowered his head and shook it. He shuffled his feet, the scrape of his chains on the deck grating at Virginia's heart.

"Papa," she whispered.

Jamie held up a hand. "Doona fash yerself, lass. I'll be taking the boy."

As the boy looked up, his wide grin cracked the dried dirt on his cheeks. "Thank you, my lord."

Jamie winced. "Mr. Munro, it is. We'll have none of that lordy talk aboot here. Welcome to America." He extended a hand, which the boy timidly accepted. "What is yer name, lad?"

"George Peeper, sir."

"Father." Virginia tugged at the sleeve of his blue serge coat. "Can we afford any more?"

Jamie Munro's eyes widened and he blinked at his daughter. "More? Just an hour ago, ye upbraided me aboot the evils of purchasing people, and now ye want more? 'Tis no' like buying ribbons for yer bonny red hair."

"I know, but this is important." She leaned toward him. "Do you see the tall man in lavender silk?"

Jamie's nose wrinkled. "Aye. Who could miss him?"

"Well, he wanted to purchase me—"

"*What?*"

She pressed the palms of her hands against her father's broad chest as he moved to confront the dandy. "'Twas a misunderstanding. Please."

His blue eyes glittering with anger, Jamie clenched his fists. "Let me punch him for you, lass."

"No, listen to me. I fear he means to buy one of those ladies for . . . immoral purposes."

Jamie frowned at her. "And what would ye be knowing of a man's immoral purposes?"

"Father, I grew up on a farm. I can make certain deductions, and I know from the way he looked at me, the man is not looking for someone to scrub his pots."

"What can I do aboot it?"

"If he decides he wants one, you could outbid him."

"He would just buy another, Ginny. I canna be buying the whole ship. I can scarcely afford this one here."

She bit her lip, considering. "You could buy one more if Aunt Mary pays for George. She can afford it much more than we."

"Nay." Jamie shook his head. "I willna have my sister paying. This is the least I can do to help Mary before we leave.

Besides, I seriously doubt I could outbid the dandy even once. Look at the rich way he's dressed, though I havena stet clue why a man would spend good coin to look like that."

The ship rocked suddenly, and Virginia held fast to her father's arm. A breeze wafted past her, carrying the scent of unwashed bodies. She wrinkled her nose. She should have displayed the foresight to bring a scented handkerchief, though not as overpowering as the one sported by the lavender popinjay.

Having completed his leisurely perusal of the women, Mr. Stanton was now conversing quietly with a young boy.

"Look, Father, that boy is so young to be all alone. He cannot be more than ten."

"Aye," Jamie replied. "We can only hope a good family will be taking him in."

"How much for the boy?" Mr. Stanton demanded in a loud voice.

The captain answered, "You'll be thinking twice before taking that one. He's an expensive little wretch."

Mr. Stanton lowered his voice. "Why is that?"

"I'll be needing payment for his passage *and* his mother's. The silly tart died on the voyage, so the boy owes you fourteen years of labor."

The boy swung around and shook a fist at the captain. "Me mum was not a tart, ye bloody old bugger!"

The captain yelled back, "And he has a foul mouth, as you can see. You'll be taking the strap to him before the day is out."

Virginia squeezed her father's arm. "The boy is responsible for his mother's debt?"

"Aye." Jamie nodded. "'Tis how it works."

Mr. Stanton adjusted the lace on his sleeves. "I have a fancy to be extravagant today. Name your price."

"At least the poor boy will have a roof over his head and food to eat." Virginia grimaced. "I only hope the dandy will not dress him in lavender silk."

Jamie Munro frowned. "Oh, dear."

"What is it, Father?"

"Ye say the man was interested in you, Ginny?"

"Aye, he seemed to like me in his own horrid way."

"Hmm. Perhaps the lad will be all right. At any rate, 'tis too late now. Let me pay for George, and we'll be on our way."

An Excerpt from

TURN TO DARKNESS
by Jaime Rush

Enter the world of the Offspring with this latest novella in
Jaime Rush's fabulous paranormal series.

CHAPTER ONE

When Shea Baker pulled into her driveway, the sight of Darius's black coupe in front of her little rented house annoyed her. That it wasn't Greer's Jeep, and that she was disappointed it wasn't, annoyed the hell out of her.

Darius pulled out his partially dismantled wheelchair from inside the car and put it together within a few seconds. His slide from the driver's seat into his wheelchair was so practiced it was almost fluid. He waved, oblivious to her frown, and wheeled over to her truck. "As pale as you looked after hearing what Tucker, Del, and I went through, I thought you'd go right home." He wore his dark blond hair in a James Dean style, his waves gelled to stand up.

She *had* been freaked. Two men trying to kill them, men who would kill them all if they knew about their existence. She yanked her baseball cap lower on her head, a nervous habit. "I had a couple of jobs to check on. What brings you by?" She hoped it was something quick he could tell her right there and leave.

"Tucker kicked me out. I think he feels threatened by me,

because I had to take charge. I saved the day, and he won't even admit it."

None of the guys were comfortable with Darius. His mercurial mood shifts and oversized ego were irritating, but the shadows in his eyes hinted at an affinity for violence. In the two years he'd lived with them, though, he'd mostly kept to himself. She'd had no problem with him because he remained aloof, never revealing his emotions, even when he talked about the car accident that had taken his mobility. Unfortunately, when he thought she was reaching out to him, that aloofness had changed to romantic interest.

"Sounded like you went off the rails." She crossed her arms in front of her. "Look, if you're here to get me on your side, I won't—"

"I'd never ask you to do that." His upper lip lifted in a sneer. "I know you're loyal only to Tucker."

She narrowed her eyes, her body stiffening. "Tuck's like a big brother to me. He gave me a home when I was on the streets, told me why I have extraordinary powers." That she'd inherited DNA from another dimension was crazy-wild, but it made as much sense as, say, being able to move objects with her mind. "I'd take his side over anyone's."

"Wish someone would feel that kind of loyalty to me," Darius muttered under his breath, making her wonder if he was trying to elicit her sympathy. "I get that you're brotherly/sisterly." He let those words settle for a second. "But something happened with you and Greer, didn't it? What did he do, grope you?"

"Don't be ridiculous. Greer would never do something like that."

"Something happened, because all of a sudden the way you looked at each other changed. Like he was way interested in you, and you were way uncomfortable around him. Then you sat all close to me, and I know you felt the same electricity I did."

She shook her head, sending her curly ponytail swinging over her shoulder. "There was no electricity. Greer and I had a . . . disagreement. I needed to put some space between us, but when you live in a house with four other people, there isn't a lot of room. When I sat next to you, I was just moving away from him."

Darius's shoulders, wide and muscular, stiffened. "You might think that, Shea. You might even believe it. But someday you're going to realize you want me. And when you do, I want you to know I can satisfy you. When I'm in Darkness, I'm a whole man." That dark glint in his eyes hinted at his arrogance. "I'm capable of anything."

Those words shivered through her, but not in the way he'd intended. In that moment, she knew somehow that he *was* capable of anything. Darius might be confined to a wheelchair, but only a fool would underestimate him, and she was no fool. Especially where Darkness was concerned. The guys possessed it, yet didn't know exactly what it was. All they knew was that they'd probably inherited it, along with the DNA that gave them extraordinary powers, from the men who'd gotten their mothers pregnant. It allowed them to Become something far from human.

"Please, Darius, don't talk to me about that kind of thing. I'm not interested in having sex with anyone."

The corner of his mouth twisted cruelly. "Don't you like

sex? Maybe you've never been with someone who could do it well."

For a long time the thought of sex had coated her in shame and disgust. Until that little incident with Greer, when she'd had a totally different—and surprising—reaction.

"Look, I'm sorry Tuck kicked you out, but I don't have a guest bedroom."

"I'll sleep on the couch. You won't even know I'm here." His face transformed from darkly sexual to a happy little boy's. "I don't have any other place to stay," he added, building his case. "You just said how grateful you are to Tuck for taking you in. I'm only asking for the same thing."

Damn, he had her. As much as she wanted to squash her feelings, some things did reach right under her shields. And some people . . . like Greer. Now, Darius's manipulation did. "All right," she spat out, feeling pinned.

Her phone rang from where she'd left it inside her truck.

"Thanks, Shea," Darius said, wheeling to his car and popping the trunk. "You're a doll."

She got into her truck, grabbing up the phone and eyeing the screen. Greer. She'd been trying to avoid him since moving out three months before. But with the weirdness going on lately, she needed to stay in the loop.

"Hey," she answered. "What's up?"

"Tuck and Darius had it out a while ago. Darius has this idea about being the alpha male, which is just stupid, and Tuck kicked him out. I wanted to let you know in case he shows up on your doorstep pulling his 'poor me' act."

"Too late," she said in a singsong voice. "Act pulled—very well, I might add. He's staying for a few days."

"Bad idea." Always the protective one. He made no apologies for it either.

She watched Darius lift his suitcase onto his lap and wheel toward the ramp he'd installed for wheelchair access to her front door. "Well, what was I supposed to do, turn him away? I don't like it either."

"I'm coming over."

"There's no need . . ." She looked at the screen, blinking to indicate he'd ended the call. ". . . to come over," she finished anyway.

She got out, feeling like her feet weighed fifty pounds each, and trudged to the door. All she wanted was to be alone, a quiet evening trimming her bonsai to clear her mind.

There would be no mind-clearing tonight. There'd be friction between Greer and Darius, just like there had been before she'd moved out. Tuck had eased her into the reality of Darkness, he and Greer morphing into black beasts only after she'd accepted the idea. Tuck told her it also made them fiercely, and insanely, territorial about their so-called mates. She hadn't thought twice about that until Darius and Greer both took a different kind of liking to her. She was afraid they'd tear each other's throats out, and she wasn't either of their mates.

"Two days," she said, unlocking her front door. "I like living on my own. Being alone." Most of the time. It was strange, but she'd sit at her table in the mornings having coffee (not as strong as Greer's k iller brew) and be happy about being alone. Then she'd get hit with a wave of sadness about being alone.

See how messed up you are.

"You might like having me around," he said. "If that guy

who's been creeping around makes an appearance, I'll kick his ass."

"Well, he's too much of a coward to knock on the door." She didn't want to think about her stalker. He hadn't left any of his icky letters or "gifts" in a few days.

She figured out where Darius could stash his suitcases and was hunting down extra sheets and a blanket when the doorbell rang. Before she could even set the extra pillow down to answer, she heard Darius's voice: "Well, look who's here. What a nice surprise."

Not by the tone in his voice. Damn, this was so not cool having them both here. They'd been like snarling dogs the day everyone had helped her move in here. She hadn't had them over since.

She walked out holding the pillow to her chest like a shield. Greer's eyes went right to her, giving her a clear *Is everything all right?* look.

She wasn't in danger. That's as far as she'd commit.

Greer closed the door and sauntered in, as though he always stopped by. "Thought I'd check in on you. After what happened, figured you might be on edge." There he went again, sinking her into the depths of his eyes. They were rimmed in gray, brown in the middle, the most unusual eyes she'd ever seen. And they were assessing her.

"She's fine," Darius answered as she opened her mouth. "I'm staying here for a couple of days, which will work out nicely . . . in case she's on edge." His unspoken *So you can go now* was clear.

Greer moved closer to her, putting himself physically between her and Darius. He was a damned wall of a man, too, way tall, wide shoulders, and just big. He purposely blocked Darius's view of her.

She'd done this, sparked them into hostile territory. Which was laughable, considering what she looked like: baggy pants and shirt, cap over her head, no makeup. She'd done everything she could for the last six years to squash every bit of her femininity. Her sexuality. Then Greer had blown that to bits.

He hadn't knocked, just barged into the bathroom, a towel loosely held in front of his naked body. She was drying her hair and suddenly he was standing there gaping at her.

"Jesus, Shea, you're beautiful," he'd said, obviously in shock.

She couldn't move, spellbound herself, which was ridiculous because she wasn't interested in anyone sexually. But there stood six feet four of olive-skinned Apache with muscled thighs and a scant bit of towel covering him. And the way he'd said those words, with his typical passion, and his looking at her like she *was* beautiful and he wanted her, woke up something inside her.

Breaking out of the spell and wrapping her towel around her, she'd yelled at him for barging in, stepping up close to him and jabbing her finger at his chest.

And what had he done? Lifted her damp hair from her shoulders, hair she never left loose, his fingers brushing her bare shoulders. "Why do you hide yourself from us?" he'd asked.

"Don't say anything about this to anyone." Would he tell them how oversized her breasts were? Would they wonder why she hid her curves, talking behind her back, speculating? "Leave. Now."

He'd shrugged, his dark brown eyebrows furrowing. "No

need to get mad or freaked out. It was an accident. We're friends."

He left, finally, and she looked in the steamy reflection. She didn't see beautiful. But she did see hunger, and even worse, felt it.

"How's your big job coming?" Greer asked now, pulling her out of the memory. He was leaning against the back of the couch, which inadvertently flexed the muscles in his arms.

He remembered, which touched her even if she didn't want to be touched. Still, she found herself smiling. "Great. We're putting the finishing touches now that the hard-scaping and most of the planting is finished. This is my biggest job yet. My business has kept me sane through all this. Gotta keep working on the customer's jobs." She glanced to the window. If the sun weren't going to be setting soon, she'd come up with some job she had to zip off to right then.

Dammit, she missed Greer. Hated having to shut him out. Now, things were odd between them. He looked at her differently, heat in his eyes, and hurt, too, because he didn't understand why she'd pushed him away. Like he'd said, it was an accident that he'd walked in on her.

"Do you want to stay for dinner?" she asked, not sure whether having them both there would be better than being alone with Darius.

Greer glanced at his watch. "Wish I could. My shift starts in an hour."

Darius wheeled up. "Yeah, the big bad firefighter, off to save lives." He made a superhero arm motion, pumping one fist in the air.

Greer's mouth twisted in a snarl. "I'd rather do that than tinker with computer parts all day."

"Boys," she said, sounding like a teacher.

Another knock on the door. Hopefully it was Tucker. He was good at stepping in. But it wasn't Tucker. Two men stood there, their badges at the ready. "Cheyenne Baker?" one of them asked.

She nodded, feeling Greer step up behind her.

"Detective Dan Marshall, and Detective Paul Marron. May we come in?"

"What's this about?" Greer asked before she could say anything.

"We have some questions about a recent incident." The man, in his forties, waited patiently for someone to invite them inside.

Greer inspected the badge, nodded to her. It was legit.

Shea checked it, too, then stepped back, bumping into Greer. "These are friends of mine," she said, waving to Greer and Darius.

Marshall closed the door behind them, taking in both men as though noting their appearance. He focused on her. "You've heard about the man who was mauled two nights ago?"

Her mouth went dry. How had they connected that to her? Bad enough that it triggered two men from the other dimension to hunt down their offspring. "Yes, it sounded horrible." She shuddered, and didn't have to fake it. "Wild animals attacking people in their own home."

"We don't think it was a wild animal. Do you know Fred Callahan, the victim?"

"No, I—" Her words jammed in her throat when she saw the picture he held up, a driver's license photo probably. All the blood drained from her face. "I knew him as Frankie C." She cleared the fuzz from her voice. "I haven't seen him for six years." She wanted the cops to go, or for Greer and Darius to leave. "I'm sorry, I can't help you."

Marshall's eyes flicked to Greer and Darius before returning to her. "We found pictures and notes about you on his computer. There was a letter in his desk drawer addressed to you, indicating he'd written to you before. It wasn't a very nice letter."

Her knees went weak. Greer somehow sensed it and clamped his hands on her shoulders. "What are you insinuating?" His hands started warming her, one of his psychic abilities.

Darius wheeled closer. "You can't possibly think this slip of a girl could tear a man apart."

"I've been getting letters, creepy gifts," she said. "But I didn't know who they were from." Frankie. She had wondered, yes, but how had he found her? And why after all these years?

"May I see them?" Marshall asked.

She'd wanted to throw them away, but thought they might be evidence if things escalated. She went to the file cabinet in her office and returned with the letters, and the box.

Marshall frowned when he opened it and saw the dildo, the flavored lube creams. "Can I take these?"

"Please." *And go. Say no more.*

He looked at Greer and Darius. "Did either of you know who was harassing her?"

Darius snorted. "No, but I'm glad the sick fu—the guy is dead. It's wrong to harass a woman like that."

Greer shook his head, but his gaze was on her.

Marshall turned to her again. "Callahan worked at the phone company. That's probably how he found you. You haven't heard from him at all in the six years since you filed charges against him and the other two men?"

"No, nothing," she said quickly. "I'd rather not—"

"I'm sure the detective you spoke to talked you out of going forward with the charges. I read the file and agree that it was a long shot to prosecute the case successfully. Still, I wish we had. One of those other men raped a teenaged girl a couple of years back. He's in prison now. The other's been jailed a few times on battery charges."

She felt Greer's questioning stare on her. "I'm sorry to hear that." Her words sounded shaky. *Leave, dammit.*

Marshall glanced in the box, then her. "But Callahan hasn't had another brush with the law. We did find some rather disturbing items in his home, including sex toys I presume he intended to send to you. One was a pair of handcuffs, and they weren't the fuzzy kind. It's the sort of thing that makes me uncomfortable about where he was going with this. So if you"—he looked at her friends—"or anyone had something to do with his death, it may have saved your life. But still, we have to investigate. It's a crime to tear a man apart, no matter how much of a scumbag he is."

"Son of a bitch," Greer said. His hands tightened on her as she slumped against the couch, and then he pulled her against his body, his arms like a shield over her collarbone.

Oh, God. Had Frankie been planning to rape her again? That overshadowed anything else in her mind at the moment.

Marshall seemed to be giving them time to fess up.

"We didn't know who the guy sending that stuff was," Shea said. "You can see from the letters that he never signed them." They'd been crude letters, detailing what he wanted to do to her body, and she'd forced herself to read them because she needed to know how much he knew about her. Or if they contained an explicit threat.

"Was it because of your earlier experience that you didn't report the stalking?" Marshall asked.

She shrugged, though it felt as though she wore an armored suit that smelled of a citrus cologne. "I didn't see it as threatening. Only gross and annoying."

Wrapped in Greer's embrace, she felt safe in a sea of chaos.

Marshall gave her his business card. "If there's anything else you know or remember, please give me a call." He took a step toward the door but turned back to her. "Ms. Baker, if anyone ever hurts you like that again, call me."

As soon as he left, Darius wheeled in front of her. "The guy's dead, Shea. You don't have to worry about him anymore. Isn't that great?"

Thank God Darius hadn't asked for more information. If only Greer would let it go.

He turned her to face him. "What happened? What was he talking about, if you're hurt 'again'?" His concern turned her to mush, and then his expression changed. He cradled her face, and as much as she wanted to push away, she couldn't. "Oh, Shea."

She heard it all in his voice—that he'd figured it out from

the detective's words. Raped "another" woman. She felt her expression crumple even though she tried to hold strong.

He pulled her against him, stroking her back. Her cap's brim bumped against him and it fell to the floor.

No, she had to push away. She would fall apart right here, and he would continue to hold her and soothe her, and it felt so good because no one had done that afterward. Not even her mother, who had the same opinion the cops did: that she deserved it.

She managed to move out of his embrace by reaching for her cap. She shoved it onto her head, pulling down the brim. "I'm fine. It was a long time ago."

"What are you two talking about?" Darius asked. At least he hadn't gotten it.

That was the difference between them, one of many. She wondered if Darius just had no emotions, nothing to squash or tuck away.

"You'd better go," she said to Greer, her voice thick. "You don't want to be late for your shift."

He was looking at her, probably giving her the same look he'd been giving her since the bathroom incident. The *Why are you shutting me out?* one. She couldn't tell, thankfully, because the brim of her cap blocked his eyes from view. At least he'd also pushed back after the bathroom incident and gone on, continued dating. He'd been cool to her afterward. That's what she wanted. Even if it stuck a knife in her chest.

"I do have to go. Walk me out." He took her hand, giving her no choice but to be dragged along with him.

The air was even more chilling now that the sun was setting. He paused by his Jeep, turning her to face him. "Shea, that's why you hide yourself, isn't it? Why you freaked when I accidentally saw you naked." He pulled off her cap. "Three of them?" His agony at the thought wracked his face.

"I don't want to discuss this. I freaked because I don't want people to see me naked."

"Because you've got curves—"

She pressed her hand over his mouth, feeling the full softness of it. "I am not interested in discussing my curves or my past."

"You're hurting, Shea. It's why you shut down on me. I lost a friend once, because he was hurting, too. Holding in a painful secret. I left for a while, doing construction out of town, and when I came back, he'd taken his life. He couldn't take the pain anymore."

"I'm not going to take my life. I've survived, gotten over it—"

"You haven't gotten over it." He tugged at her oversized shirt. "You hide your body. All those years you lived with us, you hid yourself. Did you think we'd hurt you? Attack you?"

He had no idea. "Of course not."

"That's why you were so pissed about me seeing you. Your secret was out."

That he had right. "That's ridiculous." She took the opportunity to look down at her attire, to escape those assessing eyes. "This is just how I like to dress."

He took his finger and lifted her chin. "I suddenly saw you as a woman and not just the girl who's lived with us for the past few years. Seeing you as a woman changed everything."

She smacked his arm, which probably hurt her more than him. "Then change it back. I don't want you like that."

He slowly blinked at her statement. "Is it because of what happened to you? We can work through that."

"Is he bothering you?" Darius called from the front step.

Greer muttered something very impolite under his breath, and then said, louder, "Go back in the house. We're talking."

Darius started to wheel down the ramp. "Whatever concerns Shea concerns me, too."

"I'm going in now," she said, dashing off before Darius could get close. As she suspected, he turned around and followed her back to the front step. Greer stayed by his vehicle, giving Darius a pissed look. She was glad Darius had stopped that conversation. Way too close for comfort on many levels.

"I'm fine, Greer," she called to him. "Thanks for caring. Get to work."

"Did I interrupt a tense moment?" Darius asked once he'd caught up to her, watching Greer's yellow Jeep back out. "Looked like he was harassing you. It had to do with whatever he did to you, didn't it? Tell me, and I'll make sure—"

"It's none of your business." She stalked into the house to find something for dinner, anything to get her mind off what just transpired.

It was hard to think about spaghetti or leftover steak when one question dominated her mind: how could it be a coincidence that the man who had been mauled was her rapist?